# In The Face Of Danger

# In The Face Of Danger

## Joan Lowery Nixon

BANTAM BOOKS
NEW YORK • TORONTO • LONDON • SYDNEY • AUCKLAND

For Beverly Horowitz
in friendship

IN THE FACE OF DANGER
*A Bantam Book / September 1988*

*The Starfire logo is a registered trademark of Bantam Books,
a division of Bantam Doubleday Dell Publishing Group, Inc.
Registered in U.S. Patent and Trademark Office and elsewhere.*

**Library of Congress Cataloging-in-Publication Data**

Nixon, Joan Lowery.
  In the face of danger.

  (The Orphan train quartet)
  Summary: Deeply unhappy about her family's separation
because of poverty, Megan gradually finds contentment
and purpose in her new home on the Kansas prairie with a
kind and loving adopted family.
  [1. Frontier and pioneer life—Kansas—Fiction.
2. Kansas—Fiction.   3. Great Plains—Fiction.
4. Foster home care—Fiction]   I. Title.   II. Series:
Nixon, Joan Lowery.   Orphan train quartet.
PZ7.N65In  1988        [Fic]        88-6230
ISBN  0-553-05490-2

*Published simultaneously in the United States and Canada*

PRINTED IN THE UNITED STATES OF AMERICA

0   9   8   7   6   5

# A Note From the Author

During the years from 1854 to 1929, the Children's Aid Society, founded by Charles Loring Brace, sent more than 100,000 children on orphan trains from the slums of New York City to new homes in the West. This placing-out program was so successful that other groups, such as the New York Foundling Hospital, followed the example.

The Orphan Train Quartet was inspired by the true stories of these children; but the characters in the series, their adventures, and the dates of their arrival are entirely fictional. We chose St. Joseph, Missouri, between the years 1860 and 1880 as our setting in order to place our characters in one of the most exciting periods of American history. As for the historical figures who enter these stories—they very well could have been at the places described at the proper times to touch the lives of the children who came west on the orphan trains.

Joan Lowery Nixon

# 1

JENNIFER WATCHED GRANDMA ladle hot cucumber pickles into a row of scalded glass jars. The recipe had been handed down in the family, Grandma had said. Jennifer wondered if her great-great-great-grandmother, Frances Mary Kelly, had made pickles like these.

She thought about the six Kelly children, Frances and her brothers and sisters, who had been sent west in 1860 to St. Joseph, Missouri, on a train with twenty-two orphans from New York City to find new families to care for them when their own mothers couldn't. How frightening it must have been to be placed with strangers, wondering when you'd ever see your brothers and sisters again! Jennifer shivered at the thought.

Frances had been able to keep little Petey with her, and Peg and Danny had remained together. Mike, who had been arrested for being a pickpocket and had been allowed to go west for a second chance instead of being sent to Tombs Prison, seemed to have had the spirit and gumption to take care of any situation.

But what about Megan, the gentle, shy, twelve-year-old

sister who had been taken far from the others to live on the Kansas prairie?

Jennifer's younger brother, Jeff, elbowed his way between Jennifer and Grandma, interrupting her thoughts. "Remember, Grandma," he said, "you promised to tell us Megan's story today."

With a quick twist of the wrist, Grandma fastened the last jar top tightly. "I was just thinking of that," she said. "This very recipe came to Frances Mary from Megan." Jennifer smiled at that as Grandma went on. "Let's leave the dishes until lunchtime and go out to the screened porch. There's no better time to tell you Megan's story than right now."

Jeff arrived at the porch first and sprawled in one of the big chairs, the breeze from the large floor fan ruffling the hair on top of his head.

Jennifer immediately dropped into the nearest chair, eager for Grandma to begin.

Grandma sat in the rocker and opened the journal in which Frances Mary had written about her brothers and sisters. "I'll read a little of what Frances wrote about Megan before I tell you the rest of the story," Grandma said. She cleared her throat and began.

*Maybe I worried more about Megan than any of the rest. I watched her chin tremble before she walked away, back straight and proud, hand in hand with Ben and Emma Browder, ready to face her new life without a complaint. I was heartbroken, not only because I was leaving this sister I loved so much, but because I knew that Megan unfairly blamed herself for what had happened to our family.*

*For as long as I live, I'll never forget that day in*

**2**

*New York City, more than two years before, when a horrible old woman made Megan think of herself as a bad luck penny.*

*There had been a loud, insistent knock at our door, and Megan ran to answer it. Ma and I were right behind her as she opened the door to a woman who was as dark and wrinkled as a walnut shell. Greasy strands of hair hung over her eyes.*

*"A gypsy," I heard Ma mutter under her breath.*

*From under her shawl the woman stretched out a clawlike hand, palm up. "Some coins for a poor old lady?" she whined.*

*Ma said firmly, "I'm sorry, but we have nothing for you."*

*She had started to close the door, but the woman snatched Megan's wrist. She poked a long and dirty finger into Megan's palm. "Ohhh," she sighed. "What have we here? Could it be that this child is a bad-luck penny?"*

*"None of that now!" Ma snapped. "Be on your way with that foolishness!"*

*Megan, whimpering with fear, tried to pull her hand away, but the gypsy's fingers dug into her wrist. The old woman thrust her face close to Megan's and muttered, "Bad luck will be with you and yours all the days of your life."*

*Megan screamed, and I let out a yelp and tried to pull her away from the gypsy. Ma picked up a broom and brandished it at the woman. "I said, be gone with you!" Ma shouted.*

*As she firmly shut the door, Ma gave Megan a hug and said, "Don't mind what that evil woman told you, love. It's all foolishness. She was just*

---

**3**

*trying to get back at me because I wouldn't give her money."*

*Ma went back to her sewing, but the fear remained in Megan's eyes.*

*Later I found Megan talking to Old Lorenzo with the twisted legs, who sat on street corners to beg. I knew she had been asking him about gypsies, because he whispered, "Of course gypsies can see things others can't see. Gypsies have the special gift."*

*And everyone in the Russian family down the hall became upset when Megan told them about the gypsy's visit. The grandmother crossed herself and babbled something in Russian, and Marfa, who was close to Megan's age, quickly murmured, "Grandma says be very careful. Who can tell the effect of a gypsy's curse?"*

*I pulled Megan into the hallway, urging, "Don't listen to the others. Listen to Ma. And to me. What the gypsy told you doesn't mean a thing. It's all just superstition."*

*But Megan held out her palm, as though trying to peer into it, and shuddered. "All the days of my life," she whispered.*

*When Da died, Megan blamed the gypsy's curse for bringing bad luck to the family. She had blamed it for Mike's arrest. Now she blamed it for Ma sending all of us to new homes in the West. As we were tearfully saying good-bye to one another in St. Joseph, Megan clung to my arm. "Oh, Frances, don't you see?" she said. "All the terrible things that have happened to our family are my fault— since the gypsy made me the bad-luck penny." She* hugged me tightly. *"Maybe you'll all be much better off without me."*

*"Oh, no, Megan!" I cried. But all I could do was watch her go with the Browders and send a prayer after her. I had no way of knowing what spells of evil—or good—might be waiting for Megan.*

# 2

MEGAN EILEEN KELLY sat on the high wagon seat, wedged between Emma and Benjamin Browder, and tried to keep her mind on the many things Emma was telling her. The past few hours in St. Joseph were like a nightmare that wouldn't go away. She had been chosen by the Browders from among all the others who had come west on the orphan train, but the memory of facing all those strangers—wondering if any of them would want her—and of being parted from her brothers and sisters kept surging into her thoughts, making her want to cry out in agony. Her spine as stiff as a broom handle, Megan clenched her fingers together tightly and forced herself to listen.

"You'll like your new home," Emma told her. She turned to Megan and smiled, her brown eyes sparkling under the deep curve of her sunbonnet. "It's prairie country. There's high grass as far as you can see, and the wind whispers through the grass like soft music."

Megan gave a little nod that was supposed to show polite interest and tried unsuccessfully to smile. *Oh,*

*Frances*, she thought, *you have Petey with you, and Danny and Peg are together. Mike can make his way anywhere. But I'm alone, without a brother or sister nearby to comfort or cling to, and I'm so terribly afraid.*

Ben, who was stocky and broad-shouldered, lightly held the horses' reins with hands that were brown and callused. "Someday you'll see miles of wheat and corn on the land instead of grass," he said. "We're helping the country grow."

There was a pause. Megan knew she was supposed to answer, but her throat was tight with the tears she was holding back, and words wouldn't come.

Emma chattered on. "In spite of the dry years, we've kept up a good-size vegetable garden in back of the house. Have you ever seen vegetables growing?"

Mutely Megan shook her head.

"It's a wonderful feeling to make something good grow from seed. In the early spring you can help plant. What vegetables do you like? Peas? Lettuce? Cabbage?"

*Cabbage—boiling in the pot with potatoes. How often have I cooked cabbage and potatoes for the family?* Megan wondered. They'd gathered around the table in the one room that had been home for as long as she could remember. Ma would dish the food onto their plates and bend her head as she said the blessing, her hair shining red-gold in the lamplight. *Oh, Ma!* Megan struggled to keep from crying out. *I miss you so much I can't bear it!*

Emma was waiting for her to speak. Megan took a deep breath, concentrated on watching the wide, dark brown rumps of Jimbo and Jay, the horses pulling the wagon, and managed to murmur, "I know how to cook cabbages."

She caught the pleased glance Emma and Ben ex-

**7**

changed. Ben was like a solid block of wood, Emma rounded like a soft pillow. To Megan they seemed so healthy, so vibrant with energy. *I wonder if Ma and Da were like that when they left Ireland and planned their new life in the United States*, Megan thought. *Could Da have been just as strong and tanned as Ben? Could our family have stayed together?* She shuddered as she remembered the gypsy's words. *"Bad luck to you and yours all the days of your life."* What chance had any of them with a bad penny in the family?

Emma was speaking again, her voice bubbling with delight. "Our dog, Lady, is going to have puppies soon. We'll find homes for all the puppies except one. One of them will be yours. And you can choose."

Megan blinked and looked up, astonished. "A puppy?" she blurted. "For me?"

"Only for you. Have you ever had a dog?"

Megan shook her head.

"Then you have a treat in store for you. A dog can be your best friend."

*Best friend?* Megan sighed. *Frances has always been my best friend, and she always will be, even though I may never see her again.*

As the wagon rolled steadily on, the road began to rise through low, rolling hills covered with golden grasses rippling and shivering in the afternoon breeze. Megan became aware that Emma had stopped chattering about Lady and the puppies she'd have. To fill the silence, Megan said the first thing that came into her mind. "I can share the puppy with your baby."

Ben's eyebrows rose, and Emma's hands went to her rounded stomach. She blushed and murmured, "Why, thank you, Megan."

Hadn't they realized she'd know what Emma's roundness

**8**

meant? She was twelve years old, no longer a child. A bird skittered up from the grasses and sailed out of sight, its cry like the wail in Megan's heart. "I'm very good at helping with babies," she said. "I have two younger—had two—" Her voice trailed off, sucked down into the hard lump that nearly closed her throat. *Why, oh why, had Ma given all her children away?*

"You'll have a better life than I can give you," Ma had told them. Megan hadn't really understood. How could life be better without Ma there to comfort and hug and laugh with them? All of them had begged to stay with her, but she had given them no choice.

Emma's left arm, warm shawl and all, enfolded Megan's shoulders. "We'll stop with friends for the night," she said, "but their house is still a long drive away. Why don't you just snuggle against me and take a little nap? You've been through a great deal today. I know you must be very tired."

Shyly Megan rested her head against Emma's shoulder. Emma tenderly smoothed back her hair, but Megan's spine and shoulders refused to relax. If she let go even for a minute, she would drown in the misery the gypsy had brought upon her and everyone she loved. *It isn't fair to the Browders*, Megan thought drowsily. *Should I warn them about the bad luck I carry with me? Should I tell them to send me back? But if they did, where would I go? What would happen to me?*

Hands gripped together tightly in her lap, Megan fell into the blurry world of half-sleep. Ben's and Emma's voices murmured over her like a blanket, and the wagon swayed and jounced with a comforting rhythm that shook away any dreams that might have come to taunt her.

Megan opened her eyes, shifting and stretching, to

discover that the sun was low in the orange-streaked sky, and the wagon was bumping along a deeply rutted lane that wound upward. At the top of the low hill, drenched in the golden light, was a small cabin. Megan rubbed her eyes and stared. There was grass growing on the roof and a small goat nibbling at the grass!

A slender woman burst from the cabin and ran toward them. Two young towheaded children streaked after her, shouting and laughing. A man strode quickly from a barn beyond the cabin to join the others.

"Nelda!" Emma Browder cried. As soon as Ben reined Jimbo and Jay to a stop, Emma leapt down from the wagon and hugged her friend. "And this is Megan, who has come to be a part of our family!" Emma said.

Megan took Emma's hand and carefully climbed over the wagon wheel to jump to the ground. The woman, who was dressed in faded brown cotton, her pale hair twisted into a knot on top of her head, was studying Megan, and the two children were openly staring. Megan could feel herself blushing, but Emma gave her a reassuring hug and said, "Megan, this is my good friend, Mrs. Parson, and the children are Teddie and Dorothea Parson."

The little girl took her thumb from her mouth and announced, "Papa and Mama call me Thea." Megan's heart gave a lurch as she remembered Peg at that age.

Will Parson and Ben, deep in conversation, led the team to the barn. Megan could hear snatches of conversation: "The election—it's all anyone talks about. River traffic? You heard about the explosion on the side-wheeler *Lillyanne*. Lost all cargo and—"

Mrs. Parson smiled broadly and reached for Megan's hand. "Come into the house," she said. "The men will bring your things from the wagon." Over her shoulder she said to Emma, "The meal will be a simple one, but filling. I know you're hungry."

As soon as the door had closed behind them, Emma helped Megan off with her coat. "I brought you a length of cloth—turkey red, as you wanted," she said to her friend, and Mrs. Parson clapped her hands in delight.

The children continued to stare at Megan as she looked around the cabin. It was only one room, and in a way that was comforting, because it was like their home with Ma in New York City. This room was much larger than her family's room in New York City and the walls were of logs with clay stuffed in all the chinks and hollows. There were two windows, one facing the front and one the back. A huge iron stove stood next to a large open fireplace at the center of the front wall. Cooking tools hung on hooks near the stove, and a large wooden cupboard, a table, and a number of wooden chairs were placed nearby. At the opposite end of the room, there were two wide beds, bright with multicolored quilts and something intricate in a frame hung on the wall. Megan walked over to see what it was. She recognized the alphabet and numbers embroidered in cross-stitch. There were words, too, but Megan couldn't read them.

She heard Mrs. Parson's voice from behind her. "Our daughter, Alice, made that sampler when she was ten. She was always so careful with her work. I've never seen cross-stitch done any better."

Megan glanced around. "Where is Alice?"

For just an instant shadows darkened Mrs. Parson's eyes as she answered, "It was a bad winter last year, and many of the children nearabouts were ill. We lost Alice."

"I—I'm sorry," Megan stammered. She hadn't meant to hurt Mrs. Parson. Too embarrassed to know what to say

**11**

or do, Megan blindly, frantically bolted out the door and around to the back of the house, taking refuge in the privy, where she leaned her head against the rough plank wall. She couldn't cry. She mustn't cry. All the sorrow had to be locked away, where it couldn't hurt.

As soon as she had composed herself, she came out of the privy. At the side of the house was a bench with a basin of cold water. Megan splashed water onto her face and dried it with the coarse towel made from rough cotton sacking that hung on the nail over the bench.

Ben, coming from the barn with Will Parson, gave her a friendly wave. Megan waved back and hurried toward the door to the house, leaving the men to splash and sputter noisily as they washed with the chilled water.

Neither Emma nor Mrs. Parson remarked on Megan's absence, but Megan could tell they'd been talking about her. Of course Mrs. Parson would be curious.

The table was already set. After everyone had gathered and a blessing had been said, the two women carried heaping plates to the table. Megan recognized the sausages, but there was an unfamiliar dark green, soft, leafy vegetable and a platter of something that Emma told her was fried patties made from cornmeal mush, served with cane syrup to pour over them. Each of the children was given a tin cup filled with milk. Megan gulped hers down greedily, and the cup was immediately refilled.

After supper, a full stomach, the fire crackling in the fireplace, and the easy chatter of both families comforted Megan. In spite of the nap she'd had in the wagon and the strange surroundings, Megan found it difficult to keep her eyes open.

Teddie yawned widely and noisily. Megan was grateful

when his mother said, "My goodness' sakes! It's time to tuck these children into bed."

Pallets were laid on the floor for the three of them; the adults would have the two beds. Megan snuggled under her quilt, tugging it around her ears, shutting out the murmur of voices and the occasional snap of breaking wood in the embers of the fire. Her eyelids were too heavy to keep open, so for the first time since the day before, on the train, Megan allowed herself to relax. She fell asleep immediately.

In her dreams she found herself at home in New York City, with the familiar, well-worn door to their room ahead of her. She reached out to grasp the knob.

"Don't open it!" she heard Frances saying.

"I have to open it," Megan answered. Trembling with dread, she turned the knob and opened the door.

Standing before her was the gnarled old gypsy woman.

Megan was unable to move as the woman came closer and closer, a finger pointed at Megan's face. "Bad penny, bad penny," the gypsy cackled.

Megan's feet were firmly fixed to the floor. She tried to cover her ears, but her arms wouldn't budge. She couldn't even turn her head. Her eyes fixed on the old woman, Megan watched her hobble into the room. The long bony finger set off whirlwinds everywhere it pointed, and one by one Megan saw her brothers and sisters disappear. Ma rushed toward the gypsy, but the whirlwind captured Ma, too, and there was no one left in the room but the old woman and Megan.

"Bad penny," the gypsy repeated. "Look what's happened to your family!"

Now Megan found herself able to move. She grabbed for the gypsy, screaming over and over, "Give them back! Frances! Ma! Where are you?"

---

**13**

Strong arms enfolded her, and she fought against them, sobbing, "Help me, Ma! Come back and help me!"

"Megan! Megan! It's all right. You had a bad dream, dear. It's all right."

Megan knew the voice. She'd heard it before. It was a kind, soothing voice. Emma's voice. She opened her eyes.

Someone had lit a lamp, and the light shone on Emma's long hair, which was down around her shoulders. "Dear little Megan," Emma said. "Hush, hush. We're here."

"The gypsy!" Megan stammered. "The gypsy came back and took my mother!"

"It was only a dream. Your mother is safe and sound."

"She has a mother? Living?" Megan heard the bewilderment in Mrs. Parson's voice.

"It wasn't Ma's fault." Megan felt a tear roll to the end of her nose. "Ma wanted us to have a better life than she could give us, so she gave us away!" A flood of tears crashed through the barrier Megan had built and spilled down her cheeks.

As though she were a baby, Megan clung to Emma and wept against her shoulder, until finally all the tears were gone. She raised her head to see tears glistening on Emma's cheeks, too.

"Oh, Megan," Emma said, "we *will* try to make life better for you."

Megan struggled to pull away from Emma and shook her head. "No," she insisted. "I'm bad luck. Something bad will happen if I stay with you. You must send me back."

Ben's face appeared above Megan, and one of his hands rested on Emma's shoulder. "You had a bad dream, and it's frightened you," he said. "That's all."

"But the gypsy—" Megan began.

"We chose you because we wanted you," he said, "and we're not going to send you back."

Emma gave Megan another hug and helped her lie back on the pallet, tucking the quilt around her snugly. "Forget the gypsy in your dream," she said. "She'll never bother you again."

The lampwick was snuffed out, and soon the house was silent. Megan lay on her back, staring into the darkness. Ma hadn't believed in the gypsy's curse either, but look what had happened: Da gone, the family scattered. It hadn't been Ma's fault. It hadn't been Mike's. The bad luck had come from the gypsy through Megan. What if bad luck now came to Emma or Ben?

Megan's bout of weeping left her too exhausted to struggle with her worries any longer. As calm now as the cool night air after a storm had passed, Megan slid into a dreamless, restful sleep.

# 3

IN THE MORNING after breakfast Ben pushed back from the table and announced that it was time to make ready to go.

While Ben and Will hitched the horses to the double-tree, Emma and Megan helped Nelda wash dishes and put away the pallets. Thea followed Megan's every step, staring up at her with big eyes.

Finally she tugged at Megan's skirt. "Play with me," she insisted.

Emma smiled over the quilt she was folding and gave a quick nod, so Megan took the little girl's hand and said, "All right. What would you like to play?"

"Let's play with my dolls," Thea said. She led Megan to the corner and opened a box, carefully removing short lengths of twigs, some of which were wrapped in tiny scraps of cloth. "This is the mother, and this is the father, and these are all the little children," she said, holding them out to Megan. "You be the father, and I'll be all the rest of them."

"The mother and a dozen children?"

Thea raised her chin and answered firmly, "I like them the best."

Megan chuckled, took the father doll, and held him on her lap.

"Well?" Thea said impatiently. "Have him say something."

Megan self-consciously held up the doll and spoke in a low voice. "Here I am, home again after a long, hard day's work," she said. "Where are my dear children?"

Thea shook her head. "The father doesn't say that. The father hasn't gone away from home. Don't you know? He works in the field and comes into the house for his noon dinner."

"Oh," Megan said. "I thought this father would carry bricks and build large buildings."

"What are bricks?"

Megan's jaw dropped in amazement. Then she laughed. "I guess I have a lot to learn about living on a farm."

Thea picked up two of her twig dolls and marched them toward Megan's father doll. "We want to pick berries, Papa, but we promise not to go without Mama and a hoe to kill rattlesnakes."

"Rattlesnakes!" Megan gasped.

"You know. Sometimes they curl up under the bushes," Thea explained.

Megan shivered. "I hope I never see a rattlesnake."

"No," Thea said. "Mama says, you hope a rattlesnake never sees *you*. Now—it's your turn again."

"What should he say?"

Thea scowled. "You're not very good at playing dolls."

"I'm sorry," Megan said. "I never had a doll."

But Megan felt a hand on her shoulder and looked up

to see Emma. "Time to leave. Get your coat," Emma said.

Thea scrambled to her feet as Megan stood. "Don't go," she said. "We want to play."

"We'll soon pay a visit to the Browders," her mother told her.

"When?"

"When the fall chores have been done. Maybe around Christmastime."

The door opened wide, and Ben stood in the doorway, almost filling it. "The wagon's ready. Time to say your good-byes."

Mrs. Parson ran to the cupboard, pulled open the bottom drawer, and took out a blue flowered sunbonnet. She set the bonnet on Megan's head and tied the strings under her chin. "A present for you, Megan," she said. "Oh, my, with your long dark hair, don't you look pretty!"

The bonnet was like a deep blue tunnel in front and spilled over her neck and shoulders in back. Megan ran the tips of her fingers around the edges of the brim. "Oh," she stammered, too surprised and excited to speak.

Mrs. Parson cocked her head and studied Megan. "The bonnet's a little large for you, but it will do."

"It's lovely," Emma said. "What a wonderful gift!"

"I made it for you, Emma," Mrs. Parson said gently. "It was to be your Christmas gift, but it seems that Megan has a greater need, if she's going to be riding on that wagon in the sun." She smiled at Megan. "The sunbonnet will keep away the freckles."

Megan didn't mind the smattering of tiny freckles that dotted her nose. If freckles bothered Mrs. Parson, she should meet Mike and Danny! Would she ever see a wild rash of freckles then! Forcing her thoughts back to the present, Megan fingered the bonnet again.

**18**

It was a beautiful color, and it was hers. Her very own. Shyly she murmured, "Thank you for the sunbonnet, Mrs. Parson." She wished she had a mirror so she could see what she looked like.

There was a last flurry of good-byes before Ben guided Jay and Jimbo onto the road. The morning was soft with mist that clung to the hills, silvered by the early light, and from each side birds rose and soared high. Their long trilling songs sounded to Megan almost like cries of joy.

With the sunbonnet on, Megan could only see straight ahead. She turned her head from left to right and back again as she tried not to miss a thing.

"Those are meadowlarks," Ben said. "Did you see them?"

"Two of them," Megan answered. She loosened the ties of her sunbonnet and let it hang at her back, feeling the cool morning air prickling her cheeks. She gave a contented sigh. The shivering grasses through which they passed spread out before her into the horizon and, as the sun began to burn off the mists, clumps of goldenrod gleamed brightly beside the road, reflecting the light.

Megan suddenly became aware that Emma was watching her, a twinkle in her eyes, and she fumbled with the sunbonnet, trying to pull it back over her hair.

Emma placed a hand on Megan's. "The sun's not yet high, so let the bonnet be for a while," she said. "Nelda still has some of the notions she was brought up with in Virginia, one of them being that ladies must have white, unblemished skins."

"You wear a sunbonnet," Megan said.

"That I do, because I sunburn easily. You probably will, too, and in that case you'll be glad of the bonnet."

"I took it off because there was so much to see," Megan said.

**19**

Emma smiled. "Do you find the prairie beautiful?"

"Yes, I do."

Emma's face flushed with joy and excitement. "I'm so glad that you like the prairie! You'll discover so many wonderful things about it. It's different and beautiful with each season of the year. It even changes with the time of day."

Megan peered at the rippling long grass as though trying to see through it. "Thea said there were snakes."

"Oh, dear," Emma murmured.

Ben spoke up. "There are snakes, yes. But you'll learn about them. You'll find plenty of the small, harmless garter snakes, and you'll learn to be cautious of the rattlesnakes, which are poisonous and deadly."

"Now, Ben," Emma began, "you mustn't frighten Megan."

But Ben looked at Megan carefully. "I think that Megan's one to face facts, and the fact is that out on the land we do watch for rattlers."

"I've never met up with a snake," Megan said, "but my brother Mike once showed me a drawing of a fearful big snake. He said it swallowed people."

Ben chuckled. "Brothers have a way of making their stories more exciting than they should be. No, rattlesnakes don't swallow people, but they do strike at them and bite them, and there is venom in their bite that makes people sicken and die. I'll teach you what rattlers look like and how to listen for their warning rattle."

"That's fine to know," Megan said, "but you had better tell me what to do next, too."

"Well, that's easy. You get out of the snake's way or kill it."

"How do you kill it? Thea said something about a hoe. Is that something to kill rattlesnakes with?"

"Good gracious," Emma said. "All this talk about snakes.

Wouldn't you rather talk about something else for a while?"

Megan shook her head. "I would rather talk about *anything* else, but only after I've learned how to kill rattlesnakes."

"Very well," Ben said. "A hoe is a metal blade attached to a long wooden handle. It's used to break up the soil in the garden and to tear up weeds. You can also raise it high in the air and bring it down hard on a rattlesnake, aiming—if possible—right behind its head."

"Will the hoe cut off its head?"

"Usually."

Megan shuddered at the mental image Ben's words called up, but what he said made good sense. "All right," she said. "Now we can talk about something else."

Ben chuckled. "You're the kind of woman who'll turn this wild prairie into good farmland."

"Megan's a treasure," Emma said. "We're so lucky to have her!"

*Lucky?* The gypsy cackled slyly in Megan's mind. Megan shivered and pushed the thought away, hoping that Emma hadn't noticed her distress.

"Let me tell you about your new home," Emma said. "We began in a house dug into the side of a hill. You'll see many houses like that with families living in them. But now we have a house of logs."

"Like the Parsons' house?"

"Like it, but larger. We have a big room for living—a parlor and kitchen combined—and we have two bedrooms on the side, with a front door in the parlor and a back door in the kitchen area." Emma smiled at Ben with pride. "Ben built most of it himself, with a little help from a near neighbor in putting on the roof."

"Emma did much of the caulking," Ben said. He glanced

at Megan. "Caulking means stuffing all the gaps and chinks between the logs with wet clay to keep out the cold and the winds."

Emma sighed. "There've been droughts that hurt many of the farmers, especially in the western part of the territory, so I feel we've been very lucky to have good healthy crops of corn for the past two years. We've been able to put real glass in our windows. And we have a well, so we don't have to carry water from the river."

"Didn't you need water to grow the corn?" Megan interrupted.

Again Emma glanced proudly at Ben. "Any crop needs water. Luckily some of our land is high and dry and some of it is fine bottomland near the river. Ben planted the cornfield on the bottomland, then dug a canal to bring river water to the cornfield. Ben is very clever."

"Why doesn't everyone live by the river?" Megan asked.

"Because of the mosquitoes, which swarm near the water and carry disease," Ben said. "Also, if the weather were to change and it rained hard enough and the river rose high enough, a flood could take the house. That's why our house is on a rise, a distance from the river."

"You could lose the cornfield if the river flooded."

"That's true. We have to take some chances."

Megan thought a moment and said, "It seems that you'd never be sure whether you'd have good crops or not."

"Maybe you should put your mind to the problem. I'd be ready to listen to good advice," Ben said.

His grin was teasing, and Megan smiled back, but Emma said firmly, "Megan, I haven't told you about the room where you'll sleep. There's a trundle bed in it, with a quilt pieced in a wedding ring pattern, all blues and reds. My mother made it for me when I was a child." She

---

**22**

gave a little bounce of excitement. "I know! We'll plant sunflower seeds under your window. Have you ever seen a sunflower?"

Megan shook her head, and Emma said, "Sunflowers grow wild in Kansas during the summer. They're tall, with gold faces the size of dinner plates. When you wake each morning you'll see them shining in at you like a row of bright suns."

In the distance Megan saw a small group of people coming in their direction. There were two men on horseback, and there was something dragging on the ground behind one of the horses. Other people walked beside the horses. Their clothing was strange, and as they came closer Megan could see that two of them were wrapped in blankets. The black hair, the dark skin—Megan gasped and clutched Emma's arm. "Indians!" she whispered. Mike had enjoyed terrifying the younger children with bone-chilling tales of Indian massacres. Megan had known that Indians lived out West, but she had never expected to see real Indians up close.

"They're traveling from one place to another, just as we are," Ben said evenly, but Megan, close beside him on the wagon seat, could feel his muscles tense.

"It looks like a family," Emma whispered. "Are they Kaw, do you think? Or Osage?"

Megan's eyes were drawn to the rifles held in slings at the side of the saddles. "W-will they t-try to kill us?" she managed to stammer.

"Not this group," Ben reassured her. "As I said, they're just travelers like us."

"How can that be?" Megan asked. "Mike said that Indians are savages, and they shoot arrows at people and cut off their hair, skin and all, and leave them for dead." *And steal children,* she thought, but this was too terrifying to say aloud.

---

**23**

"There've been Indian wars, and there are more to come, I'm afraid," Ben said, "but there are plenty of Indians who want only to be left alone to live in peace."

The traveling group was close to them now. Ben touched the brim of his hat and held up one hand, palm out. One of the men on horseback held his right hand up in the same gesture.

"Peace," Ben murmured.

Megan tried not to stare at the fringed and beaded jackets and leggings, the blankets wrapped around the women on foot and the old person peering out from the horse-drawn sling. Megan glanced into the eyes of a girl, probably close to her own age, that were as black as her hair. There was no expression on the girl's face, not even curiosity, and Megan wondered what the girl might be thinking.

The taller woman suddenly called out something. One of the men on horseback wheeled his horse and reined him in directly in front of the Browders' wagon, blocking their way. Unable to go forward, Ben halted his team.

"What do they want?" Emma whispered. She clutched Megan's hand so tightly that it hurt, and Megan knew Emma was afraid.

"I don't know," Ben said in a quiet voice. Megan saw him glance quickly at his rifle, which was on the floorboards near his feet.

The woman spoke to the man again, then turned and stared greedily at Megan. *This is what the gypsy meant,* Megan said to herself.

24

# 4

MEGAN CLUNG TO Emma, so terrified that for a moment she felt faint. Her ears buzzed, and pinpricks of light flashed before her eyes, blinding her. Megan was so sure that the Indian woman wanted her it took a few moments for her to realize that the Indian man on horseback had spoken only one word: "Food."

The Indian woman's gaze moved from Megan to the wagon bed, and Megan sighed with relief, slumping against Emma. The woman had probably been as curious about Megan as Megan had been about the woman's daughter.

"We have food for our own journey," Ben said. "We'll share what we have with you."

The Indians made no sign they had heard, but Ben handed the reins to Emma, then jumped from the seat and walked to the rear of the wagon. Megan turned to watch him open the hamper Mrs. Parson had packed for them and wrap half the food in a bleached sack.

Solemnly the Indian woman stepped forward and took it. The Indian on horseback waited until Ben had climbed back into the wagon, then gave a single nod of his head.

He guided his horse to the head of his group, and the others followed behind him.

Clucking at Jay and Jimbo, Ben gave the reins a flip, and they moved on. Megan twisted to glance back, wondering if the Indian girl would turn to look at her, too, but the Indians went on their way as though the meeting hadn't taken place.

"Where did they come from?" Megan whispered, even though she knew the Indians were now too far away to hear her question.

"If they were Kaws, they may have come from Council Grove, where the government has put them on a tract of land. Of course they could have been Osage, too. Kaws and Osage look alike. They're taller and better formed than the people in some of the other tribes."

"Other tribes? How many are there?"

"In the Kansas territory? Let's see, there's Pawnee, Cherokee, Wichita—" He broke off as he looked down at her. "Don't look so worried, Megan. As I said before, the Indians are people like us. Mostly, we try to get along with each other."

Megan thought again about the girl with the black eyes. "I'm glad you gave them something to eat," she said.

"Speaking of something to eat," Emma announced, "the sun's high, and I'm hungry. I'm sure Megan is, too."

"We're not far from home. Sure you don't want to just keep going?" Megan saw the twinkle in Ben's eyes. He liked to tease, the way Da had. Megan well remembered the twitch of a smile on Da's face and the way his eyes had sparkled with mischief.

Ben guided the wagon off the road, and the three of them soon demolished the rest of the cold meat and bread. As he closed the hamper, Ben glanced sideways at Emma, ducking his head a little. "Nelda had put in three apples," he said. "I gave them to the Indians."

Megan thought of the wonderful tartness of an apple, and she could almost feel the spurt of juice in her mouth. She pictured the Indian girl eating her apple and knew she should feel generous about giving and sharing, but she didn't. She wished that Ben had kept the apples.

Emma, however, simply said, "Nelda packed more food than we needed." Ben rested a hand on her shoulder, and the look that passed between them revealed their closeness and contentment with each other. As Emma began to rearrange the hamper and the bundles around it into place again, she sighed. "Times have been harder for Nelda and Will than for us, and they could little spare all this food."

Ben patted his stomach. "It went to a good cause."

Emma smiled. "We'll make it up to them when they come at Christmastime."

Megan walked a few steps into the long grass and stared out over the low hills, the noonday sun warm on her back. She breathed in deeply the pleasant, sour-sweet fragrance of the stems crushed under her feet and realized with surprise that already she felt a part of this glowing landscape. She wanted to race across the prairie and fling herself facedown, burrowing into the grasses, hugging the earth from which they grew.

"This is the prairie's golden time," Emma said beside her. "Later on, in winter, the grass will be dried and blackened, but in the spring the new grass will grow and the hills will turn green. There's wild indigo and blue-stem. And after that there's bird's-foot violets, prairie roses, daisies, and purple milkweed. And the birds!" She laughed. "They start singing at sunrise, and after the sun has gone down you'll often hear the mockingbird still trilling, as though the day hadn't been long enough to hold his song."

"You love the prairie," Megan said.

"Yes, I do," Emma answered.

"Did you ever live in a city?"

"No. I've never known city life. Ben and I both lived on farms in Indiana, but when we married we didn't have enough money to buy land there, so we came west to the open territory and found a plot of land we knew from the start should be ours."

Ben had come up beside them. "Kansas soil is black and rich. If grasses can grow eight to ten feet high in it, then think what corn and wheat could do." He gestured toward the land that lay before them. "Can you picture prosperous farms as far as the eye can see?"

"I could try," Megan said, "but if the hills were covered with farms, then the prairie would be gone."

Ben chuckled heartily. "Now, Ben," Emma chided.

"I don't mind," Megan reassured her. "Sometimes the things I said would make Da laugh, too. But he always told me he wasn't laughing at *me*, he was laughing at the rest of the world, which had no idea what was in store for it when responsible people would finally take over and set things to rights."

Ben stopped and studied her for a moment. Then he smiled and said, "Your Pa was right, Megan. And as for this land, I hope there'll be room for both farms and prairie." He turned and headed for the wagon, saying over his shoulder, "Let's get a move on. We want to show this young lady her new home."

Megan was delighted when she saw the Browders' house. It was built from logs, all the cracks between

**28**

them caulked with clay, and it had a sod-covered roof. As Emma had said, it was much larger than the Parsons' house. The door at the front overlooked the road, and the back door faced a huge barn, with a side overhang to protect the wagon. Megan remembered Da's pride in the buildings he had helped to build and knew Ben must take great pleasure in this house he had built with his own hands.

She looked at him shyly. "It's a grand fine house you have made for yourselves," she said.

Ben grinned at her. "It's your home now, too, Megan," he answered.

As they climbed down from the wagon and Ben began to unhitch the horses, they were greeted with delirious, joyful barks. Lady, a brown and white dog of mixed breed, half-waddled, half-ran to lick their fingers, wiggling and whining with pleasure.

"She's telling us she missed us," Emma said.

Megan could see how friendly Lady was, but she wasn't used to dogs and wasn't sure what she should do. As Lady finished greeting Emma and came over to carefully examine her, Megan looked to Emma for guidance.

Emma bent to stroke Lady's head. "This is Megan, Lady. You'll want to be her friend." She said to Megan, "Close your fingers, then slowly hold out the back of your hand to Lady."

As Megan did, Lady cautiously sniffed her hand. Satisfied, the dog moved forward, and Megan timidly scratched her behind the ears.

"She'll accept you now," Emma said, and she led Megan into the house, Lady following.

Just as Emma had described, there was a brightly colored quilt on the bed in the room Megan would have for her own. Her window faced the unplowed land that rolled down to the river. Megan could see the river a fair distance away, bordered by trees with tall, graceful trunks and bright splotches of golden leaves. "Beautiful," Megan whispered. She ached for the familiar crowded friendliness of that New York room, but she was not quite able to believe that this wonderful room was to be her own.

Megan soon decided, however, that the kitchen was her favorite place. She stood there admiring the wide fireplace and double swinging arms for holding kettles and pots over the embers. There was a small wood-burning stove, its black pipe disappearing through a hole in the roof, and pans and cooking tools galore hanging on the wall beside it. Oh, if Ma were only here to see this wonderful kitchen!

A sudden wave of longing for her mother swept over Megan with such force that she trembled and reached out for the back of a chair to steady herself. She had to put aside all wishful thinking and face the truth, she told herself. Ma would never see this room. It wasn't likely that she would ever be with Ma again!

Megan closed her eyes, fighting down the cry that tried to explode from the tight place in her chest. Firmly, she pushed back the tears that threatened to come, tucking the pain into a hidden corner of her mind. This was no time to give in to her feelings. There were things to busy herself with. First, she would unpack her few clothes and stack them in the drawers of the small chest next to the bed in her room. . . .

"Megan!"

She turned to see Ben at the open front door. He beckoned to her and said, "Put on your coat and come outside. I want you to meet our near neighbor, Farley Haskill. He's the one who looked after our livestock and property while we were in St. Joe."

Megan grabbed her coat from the rack that stood next to the front door and shoved her arms into the sleeves. The breeze was chill, and she pulled the coat snugly around her, as she followed Ben outside.

Farley, a short, stocky, balding man, rubbed his hands on the seat of his overalls as Megan approached, then shook her hand. "Mighty pleased to make your acquaintance," he mumbled, and Megan was surprised to perceive that he was as shy as she was. "It's nice to have a child in these parts," he added. "Nearest family with children is about three miles to the southwest."

Megan realized that she'd been counting on some neighbor nearby to have children that she could take care of and play with. It was hard to imagine life without other children around. Ben must have realized her disappointment and added, "I guess it's hard for someone from the big city to realize neighbors are far away."

"Yes," she admitted. "I was hoping you'd say that you and your wife had children, Mr. Haskill."

His eyes opened wide. Then he stared at the ground, blushing, and shifted from one foot to the other. "No," he said. "Never been married. I live alone."

"Farley's chosen to be a bachelor," Ben said, amicably clapping a hand on Mr. Haskill's shoulder.

But Megan caught a sudden, secretive spark in Mr. Haskill's eyes before he turned away. *What is he hiding?* she wondered.

The two men began talking about things pertaining to the farm, so Megan ran back into the house. Emma was busily attacking the wooden floor with a broom. "Gone four days, and the dust is an inch thick!" she said.

Megan hadn't noticed much dust, but she was good at sweeping. She had always done it for Ma. "Let me do that for you," she said.

---

**31**

Emma kept a firm grip on the broom and smiled. "I'm just letting the house know I'm back," she said. "Or maybe I'm doing this for myself, because it makes me feel that I'm home again and comfortable at settling in."

"If doing a chore does all that for you, than maybe it will do the same for me," Megan said. "Do you have something for me to do so that I'll feel at home?"

"Oh, dear little Megan!" Emma dropped the broom and enfolded Megan in a hug.

Megan, her head nestled against Emma's chest, could hear the calm, steady beat of Emma's heart and feel the thrust of her well-rounded belly against her own body. The belly suddenly gave a thump and shifted, and Megan stepped back, smiling. "When will the baby come?" she asked.

Emma gently patted the protruding curve. "Late December or early January," she said. "Nelda told me this child is so active, it's bound to be strong and healthy."

Megan could still remember when Ma's babies were born. Old Mrs. Gridley, who lived down the hall, always came to help. The first thing she did every time was to shoo the children out of the room.

When Petey, the youngest, was about to be born, Megan had begged to stay, frightened at leaving Ma. Her hair down and soaked with perspiration, Ma seemed to be in some faraway place where she could neither see nor hear her children. But Mrs. Gridley put Megan out of the room, telling her to help Frances watch Mike, Danny, and Peg.

Finally Mrs. Gridley had opened the door to invite them back inside, informing them that they had a beautiful baby brother. Megan had hung on Ma's arm, staring at the tiny round red face in the bundle Ma was holding. "I was afraid," she whispered.

Ma reached over to brush a tear from Megan's cheek. "Dear little love, having a baby is part of a woman's life, and it is surely a great waste to be afraid of life. Just look at this fine boy now. Wouldn't you say he was worth it?"

Megan pulled herself back to the present and asked Emma, "When the time comes, will there be a woman here to help you?"

"Yes, Megan. Don't worry," she said. "There is a grandmother who lives with her family in a sod house about five miles from here. She's already promised to come ahead of time and stay with us so she'll be at hand when the baby is ready."

"Good," Megan said and gave a little shiver of relief.

Ben stomped his feet on the front step, knocking the dust from his boots, and opened the door. "Megan," he said, "would you care to come outside again? I'd like to show you our farm."

"Oh, yes," Megan said. She reached again for her coat.

"Where's Farley?" Emma asked. "He is planning to stay for supper, isn't he?"

"I invited him," Ben answered, "but he was in a hurry to get home." He shook his head. "It's funny, but I get the feeling that there's something on that man's mind."

"What?" Emma asked.

"If I knew, I'd tell you," Ben said with a chuckle. "Come on, Megan. Ready?"

Megan eagerly fumbled at the last buttons on her coat. She ran to keep up with Ben as he strode toward the barn, Lady waddling alongside. The large doors were shut, so Megan followed Ben up a stone step and through a small doorway that opened over a high sill.

The barn stood empty except for a lean brown rooster who squawked loud complaints, angrily flapping past them. "That's Goliath," Ben said. "He has the run of the place and thinks he owns it all."

"Does he live here in the barn?"

"No, he shares the coop behind the barn with the other chickens."

Megan had stepped aside to give Goliath plenty of room. "Does he bite?" she asked.

"Bite, no. Peck, yes. He might try to frighten you by rushing at you with his wings flapping. Just pick up a stick or something to wave in his face and yell at him with a voice a little louder than his own. He'll turn and run, the coward that he is."

Megan smiled. "I don't know much about any kind of animal," she said.

"Then this is a good place to learn," Ben told her. He pointed out some of the pieces of equipment in the barn, then led her through a wide door at the far end that opened into a corral.

"Oh," Megan said. "There are Jay and Jimbo." The horses were busy eating at the trough. As she watched them, a shadow suddenly fell across her shoulders, and Megan turned to see a monstrous hairy face with two horns. Its gigantic eyes and snuffling nose were just a few inches from her own.

Megan screamed and stumbled backward, tripping and landing with a thump on the ground. The face—which belonged to some kind of large animal—followed her down, huge eyes staring, and Megan screamed again. Lady ran between the animal and Megan, barking furiously.

Ben grabbed one of the animal's horns and tugged it away. The animal backed and turned, nonchalantly swaying to the opposite side of the corral, and Ben lifted Megan to her feet. "That's just Rosie, our cow," he said. "She won't hurt you."

Megan, embarrassed, tried to brush off her skirt. "A cow, is it?" she asked. "I saw cows from the train, but none as huge as that."

"They'd be the size of Rosie if you saw them up close," Ben said. "Rosie's a gentle soul. She's just curious."

"Too curious for her own good."

Ben laughed. "Before long you'll take Rosie for granted. Tomorrow, if you like, I'll teach you to milk her."

Megan studied Rosie for a moment, then nodded. "I think I'd like that, if Rosie wouldn't mind."

"We won't bother to ask her," Ben said. "It's best just to tell Rosie what to do, so she won't think she's got more say-so than any cow ought to have."

Lady rubbed against Megan's legs, and Megan stooped to scratch behind her ears and under her chin. "Thank you for protecting me," Megan murmured. Lady looked up at her with such devotion that Megan had to hug her, rubbing her chin against the top of Lady's head.

"Lady will want to come with us when we walk to the river," Ben said, so Megan hopped up and followed him from the corral. As Ben had said, Lady was right at their heels.

Not far from the privy was a mound of earth high enough to have a door and one window in it. "What is that?" Megan asked.

"A root cellar now," Ben said. "A place to store the potatoes and vegetables in the winter, and a place to go for safety from tornadoes in the spring." Ben glanced down at her. Before she could ask, he explained, "Big windstorms. When a tornado comes, the safest place to be is underground. By the time tornado season gets here, you'll know all about what to do when you see a tornado coming."

Megan shook her head. "I don't want to see a tornado," she said.

"No one does, but they're a fact of life out here."

"Did you build the root cellar to get away from tornadoes or to store food?"

"We built it as a place to live," Ben said. "That was our home when Emma and I first claimed this land."

"You lived underground?" Megan shuddered.

"It wasn't that bad." Ben smiled at Megan's embarrassment. "Many of the folks who come here live in dugouts until they prosper enough to build a sod house or a log house like ours."

As they passed a small garden at the back of the house, Ben pointed out a few squash and pumpkins half-hidden among the wide-leafed, scraggly vines. "The last of the fall vegetables," he said. "In the early spring, we'll dig the ground and plant row after row of new vegetables." He swung his left arm in an arc, indicating the surrounding land. "Someday," he said, "this will be planted in wheat. I know this is good land for wheat, and there are farmers to the east who have been successful with it."

"Then why don't you grow wheat now?"

"Wheat needs enough water to nourish it, and these last few years have been dry. Seed costs money, and it takes time and care, as well as enough land, to make the seed grow. I was able to bring water to my cornfield, but so far I haven't thought of a way to carry enough river water to a prairie to make it bloom."

Ben fell silent for a while. Megan strode after him. The soft stalks of the tall grass whipped at her dress, and their dusty fragrance pricked her nostrils. She plucked the tip off one of the grasses, its already-browning buds purple and red and deep gold, and tickled it against her chin. Wouldn't little Peg and Petey love to play in this grass, which was tall enough to hide in? She could almost see them racing past her, laughing and shrieking, "I tagged you! You're it!"

Ben stopped short, and Megan broke quickly from her daydream. They were standing on a low bluff, looking down at what remained of a cornfield, dried stalks gathered in piles. Beyond the cornfield was a narrow stream that trickled down the center of a scooped-out rocky bed. On the bank of the river were clusters of the pale golden trees Megan had seen from her window. In many places their gnarled roots rose from the rocks, stretching wide.

"The trees look as if they're reaching for the water," Megan said.

"That's exactly what they're doing," Ben answered. "As you can see, this land won't support many trees. That's why so many people live in sod houses. Like Farley Haskill."

He pointed to a spot across the river.

Megan couldn't see Mr. Haskill's house until a ray of sunlight reflected off the single window by the front door. The house had been cut into the bluff overlooking the riverbank, and the only part that looked like a house was the wooden front—about eight feet wide at the most, she guessed. Built into the house front was a wooden door with a string hanging out of the latch.

"He lives in the ground, just like you did," Megan said in wonder.

"You'll see the inside when we visit Farley someday," Ben said. "The rooms are large enough, but they're dark, and the snakes and rats like to sneak in out of the heat when they get a chance. When Farley has made his farm more successful, he'll be eager to build a real house out of logs, as we have."

"He lives all by himself," Megan said. "He must be lonely."

37

"Farley's never said so, but I suppose he might be," Ben answered. "He comes by our place now and then, and Emma often takes him bread from the oven or fresh vegetables."

"Even though his house is mostly made of dirt, it looks very tidy on the outside," Megan said. "I like that bush with the bright yellow flowers that's growing next to the front door."

"Goldenrod." Ben spoke absentmindedly, rubbing his chin. "I knew something looked different. It's that goldenrod. It's been planted recently, and you're right. The yard has been cleared."

"Mr. Haskill lives very close to the river."

"Too close," Ben said. "I warned Farley about the mosquitoes, but he'd settled in this spot even before we arrived. This was his home, and he wasn't about to change it. He said he'd had one bout of the fever and wasn't likely to have another, although there's always the danger."

Megan studied the small, almost hidden spot dug in the earth and said, "'If Mr. Haskill's in danger, to my way of thinking it would be from pure loneliness."

# 5

AFTER A SUPPER of corn bread, fried bacon, and buttered squash, Ben took his two rifles from the rack on the wall and began to clean them. Megan—still rosy from a warm bath and wrapped in her nightshift and one of Emma's soft robes—curled on a chair as Emma opened a book, holding it to the lamplight, and began to read a tale about a lion and a mouse:

> *"Let me go," said the mouse, "and someday I may be of help to you."*
> *The idea that this little mouse could do anything to help a large, magnificent beast like a lion greatly amused the lion, so he let the mouse go.*

"Huh!" Megan said. "That lion had a very high opinion of himself. I hope the mouse got clear away from him and never came back."

Emma blinked with surprise. "Wait. I haven't finished the story." She read on, about the lion being caught in a hunter's net and the mouse gnawing through the net to set the lion free. "The lesson we should learn is never to belittle smaller things," she read and turned to Megan with a smile.

"Yes," Megan said, "but I do wish that the lion had told the mouse he was sorry for putting his nose in the air and trying to be so high and mighty. The lion's the one who should have learned a lesson."

"Perhaps the storyteller assumed that the lion had."

"Who was this storyteller?"

"A man named Aesop, who lived many, many years ago. Did you like the story, Megan?"

Megan thought a moment. "Yes, I did. But it was very different from the stories Ma and Da used to tell us. Their Irish stories were grand, with battles and magic and fiery pookas so frightening we'd shiver down to our toes. I don't think this Mr. Aesop was Irish, was he?"

Emma smiled. "As a matter of fact, he wasn't. But I hope you'll like his fables. We can read the rest of the book together."

Megan had already told Emma she couldn't read, because Emma had talked about reading practically the first moment they met. But she still felt embarrassed. "Frances and Mike learned to read easily," she blurted out, "but I didn't take to it the way they did."

Emma patted Megan's shoulder and smiled. "You're a bright girl, Megan, and you'll soon be reading as well as your brother and sister. Do you know any of your letters?"

"Y-yes. Those I know."

"Very well." Emma pointed to a word. "Tell me the letters in this word."

"*M* and *e*."

"Every letter has a sound of its own. *Mmmmm* is the *m* sound. You say it."

Megan did, and Emma said, "Now tell me the sound that *e* makes, and say the two sounds together."

**40**

"Eeee," Megan murmured. "Mmmmm—eeeee. Mmm-mm—Oh! *Me!*"

"That's right. The word is *me*. Do you see it anywhere else on the page?"

Megan studied the jumble of letters until she found it. Excitedly she pointed it out. "Here it is! And here again!"

"That's reading," Emma said. "Just what you were doing."

Megan joyfully hugged the book to her chest. "I'm going to learn to read!"

"And write, too," Emma said. "So you can write to your mother and to your brothers and sisters."

The room blurred as tears rushed to Megan's eyes, and she tried to rub them away.

"I know that you miss your brothers and sisters very much," Emma murmured.

Megan nodded. "I was thinking today about the little ones. We were very close, because they were in my care while Ma and Frances worked. I wonder how they're faring, and do they miss me as much as I miss them? Petey is so young. Will he forget me?"

"Of course he won't," Emma said. She put her hands on Megan's shoulders, and Megan could see the firm promise that shone in Emma's eyes. "It will be hard for us to travel during the winter, but when the spring comes, we may be able to take you to visit them."

Hope was like a warm spot burning in Megan's chest, and she hugged the book more tightly.

Ben got to his feet. He replaced the rifles in their rack and began to bank the fire, the orange glow casting deep shadows across his face. "Time for bed," he said, but as he spoke, a weird, high-pitched wail sounded somewhere outside. It seemed to come from far away, and yet its echo hung in the room as though it had seeped through the walls.

**41**

Megan gasped. "What was that?"

"Nothing to be afraid of," Ben said.

"Was it an Indian?"

Ben shook his head, and Megan stood up, still holding tightly to the book. "Then I'm not afraid," she said, adding with a touch of mischief, "unless you tell me that horrible sound came from the cow."

Emma and Ben laughed, and Ben said, "Poor old Rosie. She frightened you by being a little too curious. No, Megan, what you heard was a wolf howling at the moon, but don't be afraid. You're snug and safe in the house."

Emma put an arm around Megan. "Come along, Megan," she said. "Time for bed. We rise early, because there's much work to do." With a folded cloth protecting her hands, she picked up and wrapped one of the flat, circular stones that were lying on the hearth, carried it to Megan's bedroom, and placed it between the sheets in Megan's bed, where it would warm her feet.

Emma tucked Megan in, pulling the quilt up to her chin. "Sleep well, dear," she said and bent to kiss Megan's forehead. "Pleasant dreams."

But Megan dreamed of Ma's kiss and Ma's strong hands tucking her into bed. When she awoke in the morning, her pillow was wet from her tears.

There was much for Megan to learn about the farm, and she loved each discovery. It was like winning a prize each time she wiggled her fingers under a scolding hen and found a warm, freshly laid egg. Goliath the rooster tried to bully her, but she shouted and chased him. As he squawked and frantically flapped his wings, running away from her as fast as he could manage, Megan laughed aloud. "You old bully!" she yelled after him. "You can't get the best of *me*!"

The first time Megan approached the cow she was so frightened she could hardly breathe. Rosie turned to stare at her, and Megan backed a step away, but she spoke up to the cow in a firm voice. "Ben said you do not bite, and I intend to stay out of the way of your clumsy feet, so let's both do our best to get this job done without any mishaps."

"Sit here. Rosie will like the feel of your head resting against her side," Ben told her. "Now—move your hands like this and like this."

Megan did as he said and squealed with delight as she heard Rosie's milk squirt against the sides of the metal pail.

One evening Ben took his Henry rifle from the rack on the wall and showed Megan how to load and handle it.

"You'd probably find it easier to shoot the smaller rifle," he said. "The Henry is a bit too heavy for you now, but I usually have the smaller one with me. It's a good idea to know how to handle whatever gun is nearby in case—well, just in case of any kind of trouble."

"Indians?" Megan whispered.

"I'm not anticipating trouble with any Indians," Ben said. "It's more the wild animals I'm thinking of. Sometimes a pack of wolves comes around. And last summer, a fair piece north of us, some folks had trouble with a bear who wandered far out of his usual territory." He smiled. "I believe in being prepared. Emma knows how to handle both rifles, and soon you will, too."

There were weeks of cool dry weather interspersed with days of late Indian summer. With her sunbonnet off as much as on, Megan helped Emma weed the vegetable garden. Ben taught her to ride Jay and Jimbo, and once she got over her awe of the imposing horses, she felt very much at home on their broad backs. And in the

**43**

evenings Emma usually read a chapter from a fat novel called *Moby Dick*, before it was Megan's turn to read while Emma sewed.

Each night during the last half of October she'd pick up the collection of *Aesop's Fables* and work her way through one of the stories. While she occasionally stumbled over a word, reading began to come easier to her, and she often read an entire paragraph without stopping for Emma's help. At times she'd pause and look up, her heart thumping with excitement. "Did you hear that now? I read all the way to the end!"

"Good for you!" Emma praised Megan as she grinned with pleasure. "You're learning quickly."

"It's grand to be reading," Megan would say, and she'd practice every chance she got.

Megan often disagreed with Aesop about the point of some of the fables, but she liked the tale of the fox who tricked the crow.

"It's very funny," she told Ben, who was mending one of his boots at the kitchen table. "In this story, a crow had a bit of cheese in her beak, and the fox wanted it. Now, I would say that the fox had no business wanting what the crow had, but the crow had stolen the cheese from someone's windowsill, so she did not have my sympathy."

"I'll agree to that," Ben said.

"Well, the fox stood under the branch the crow was sitting on and began to flatter her. He told her things that no crow in her right mind would believe. Then finally he said he was sure that if she could sing she would sound like a nightingale. And do you know what that foolish crow did?"

"What?" Ben grunted as he tried to tug a thin strip of leather through a narrow hole in the side of the boot.

"Opened her beak to sing and dropped the cheese! The fox picked it up and trotted off, saying, 'I may have said many fine things about your beauty, but I never for a moment mentioned your brains!' Isn't that funny?" Megan laughed with delight.

"Yes, it is," Ben said. "I suppose the lesson is to beware of people who flatter you."

"That's what Mr. Aesop said," Megan told him. "However, he missed one or two other lessons."

Ben looked up. "What other lessons?"

"Well," she said, "for one thing, the crow should not have stolen the cheese. And for another, whoever was careless enough to leave the cheese on the windowsill in the first place deserved to lose it."

Ben began to laugh, and Megan laughed with him. "At least you found one of the fables that you like," Ben said.

Megan shrugged. "As a storyteller Mr. Aesop wasn't very exciting, but the poor man was doing his best, and we can't hold it against him that he wasn't born Irish with the natural gift."

Emma laid her sewing in her lap and asked, "Megan, could you tell us one of the Irish stories your mother and father told you?"

"I can try," Megan said. Remembering well how Da had told the story, she began: "It was a silvery night, a night in which the moon lights each pebble of the road, making the way safe for travelers. Fiona O'Fallon, who was known to be the best seamstress in the whole of Ireland, tucked her thread and packet of needles into her pocket and left a house where she had been sewing a gown for a young woman about to be married...." Just as Da had, Megan made her voice deep and impressive when she told about the meeting between Fiona O'Fallon and the Queen of the Faeries, who wanted to take her away to the fairy kingdom. "Fiona O'Fallon knew she had no power to resist the mighty Queen of the Faeries, but she had the wit to pull the thread and packet of needles from her pocket and drop them on the ground before she was carried away by a great gust of wind."

Delighted at the rapt attention Ben and Emma were giving to her story, Megan went on to tell how Fiona's son found the thread and needles, realized what had happened to his mother, and set about bringing her home again.

"So as the sound of a great wind rushed over his head, he threw into it a handful of dirt and shouted, 'I command you. Release Fiona O'Fallon!'

"His mother dropped from the cloud, almost into his arms, and praised him for his bravery and quick thinking. And oh, didn't she have much to tell her family about what she had seen and where she had been."

As Megan leaned back in her chair, Emma clapped her hands. "Wonderful!" she said. "I don't know when I've heard such an exciting story!"

"I'll tell you another tomorrow," Megan said. "About a pooka whose eyes glowed like two red-hot coals."

"Oh, Ben," Emma said, "when the Parsons come to visit, won't they love to hear Megan's stories!"

Megan ducked her head, blushing with pleasure.

She had learned to print neatly and, although she had to ask Emma how to spell many of the words, she proudly wrote four letters, one each to Ma, to Frances and Petey, to Mike, and to Danny and Peg.

The early November days grew cooler, and Megan bundled herself up against the wind that blew the grasses almost flat against the earth.

She woke one night, hearing movement and Ben's and

Emma's voices in the kitchen. It was dark. Why were they awake? It was too soon for the baby to come. Quickly Megan jumped from her bed and stumbled to the kitchen.

Emma and Ben were crouched next to Lady, who was lying on a bed they had made for her from a worn quilt. Emma looked up at Megan and smiled. "The puppies are being born," she said.

Megan tiptoed a little closer, holding her breath in awe as Ben held up a wet, pink, mewling pup.

"I thought they'd look like Lady!" Megan exclaimed. "Why is it so small? Why doesn't it have hair?"

"Give it time," Ben answered and turned his full attention to Lady as she began to whimper.

"Megan," Emma said quietly, "come and sit by me. Lady loves you. She'll be glad to know you're here."

Megan sat back on her heels, sometimes holding her breath, sometimes gasping with excitement, as three more healthy puppies were born.

Lady and the pups were moved to a large box Ben had made for them. Megan understood that she shouldn't try to touch the puppies. They were so new, so very young, and they belonged only to their mother. But some day one of them would be hers! She stroked Lady's head, scarcely able to contain her happiness.

Megan eagerly volunteered to clean the box and care for Lady, and each day she watched the puppies grow. To her delight, Emma suggested that she name them. The smallest one, with the white paws, she named Peggy. "After my little sister," she told Emma. "I just wish I could give the puppy to Peg. She's never had a dog to love."

"Maybe she does have a dog," Emma said. "I can't imagine a farm without a dog."

Megan brightened. "I'll ask her in my next letter." She picked up the two with white markings like stars on their foreheads. "This is Moby and this is Dick."

Emma smiled. "How about that fat spotted fellow who's so frisky? What are you going to name him?"

Megan picked up the wiggling pup and snuggled him close. "This is Patches," she said, "and he's mine."

Lady carefully climbed into the box, stirring and settling until she was comfortable. Megan put Patches next to her as the other pups began scrambling over each other, pushing and squirming to get their next meal. As Megan expected, Patches did his best to edge out the others. Megan grinned. She already loved him almost as much as she did Lady.

Late one afternoon, Clem Parker, who served as postmaster for the area, rode over from his farm six miles away with two letters for Megan. One was from Frances and one from Ma. Since the letters were written in script, Emma had to read them aloud to Megan.

Megan didn't mind sharing her letters with Emma. As she listened to Frances's letter, Megan could almost hear her sister saying the words aloud. Her eyes filled with tears as Emma read, "I pray, darling sister, that you are with a loving family. Sometimes I ache with missing you, and I hope we'll soon see each other again."

Emma patted Megan's shoulder, and Megan looked up to see her tears reflected in Emma's eyes. "Until I was nine I had a big sister," Emma said. "After we lost her I missed her so much I thought I would die, too. I know how much you miss your Frances."

Megan rubbed her sleeve against her eyes. "Let's read Ma's letter now," she said, and opened the thin envelope with trembling fingers.

"I have a new address," Ma wrote. "I'm working as a downstairs maid for a well-to-do family in an elegant house. I have my own cubbyhole to sleep in up in the attic, as does each of the servants in the house."

Megan's heart gave an extra thump. Ma in another house? Then the home the Kellys had lived in was gone! "Oh!" she gasped, and Emma stopped reading to look at her.

"What is it, Megan?" Emma asked.

Megan closed her eyes for a moment. Ma was living in grander style now, and shouldn't Megan be glad for it? Shouldn't she want Ma to have good food and her own room in a grand house? Of course she should. They had all known from the time they had left New York City there'd be no going back. Megan opened her eyes. "I'm all right," she said. "Please keep reading."

Emma found her place in the letter and went on again. Ma went on to describe the butler "whose nose points to the heavens" and the cook "who is round as her sauce-pans" and the upstairs maid "who puts on the greatest of airs but whistles through the gap in her teeth."

Emma burst into laughter. "Your mother is a great storyteller, too!" she said.

Finally she read Ma's parting words. "I hope you understand, love, why I did what I had to do. I love you with all of my heart and always will."

Emma looked concerned, but Megan smiled bravely. "I do understand what Ma did," she said. "I hope you do, too, because I want you to think only good things about my mother."

"Of course. I'm glad you can forgive her," Emma began, but Megan shook her head.

"There's nothing to forgive. As Ma said, she did what she had to do. She loves us, and I know she misses us as much as we miss her."

**49**

With that Megan's brave resolve vanished. She burrowed her head into Emma's lap and burst into tears.

All day Megan carried the letters in her pocket, and that night she slept with them under her pillow.

With his empty wagon rattling and clattering as it bounced on the hard-packed road, Farley Haskill arrived the next morning. It was a clear, bright day in mid-November with the sun so surprisingly warm that Megan had gladly shed her coat.

Mr. Haskill asked Ben to take care of his livestock while he traveled to St. Joseph and back. "Got to pick up some supplies afore winter sets in," Mr. Haskill stammered. He looked at his wagon, at the ground, and at the sky, but never directly at Ben or Megan.

"Is everything all right, Farley?" Ben asked.

"Of course everything's all right!" Mr. Haskill's voice cracked, and his face turned as red as Goliath's waggling comb. He climbed to the seat of his wagon and visibly tried to collect himself by gulping a couple of times. Megan was fascinated by the way his Adam's apple bobbed up and down.

"Got a lot on my mind, I tell you," Mr. Haskill said. "I just hope it works out right, but I want you to know I'm beholden to you for your help."

"That's what neighbors are for," Ben said.

"Anything you need me to get for you in St. Joe?"

"Nothing I can think of," Ben said. "We got all that we went after on our own trip to St. Joe."

"And a bit more," Farley said, and winked in Megan's direction.

With a sudden ache in her chest Megan thought about the bustling streets of St. Joseph. It was there she'd last seen Mike and Danny and Frances and Petey and Peg.

She could feel Frances's arms around her, and a sob rose in her throat. Thankful that the men were talking and hadn't noticed, Megan raced into the house.

Back in the house after the noon meal, as Emma was washing the dishes and Megan drying them, Ben told Emma about Mr. Haskill's leaving. "I never saw the man in such a stew," he said.

Emma frowned. "Do you think he's deserting his farm? Could he be giving up and going back east the way so many others have done?"

"Farley wouldn't just up and leave without saying so," Ben said. "His stock is there. I looked into his dugout to make sure it was in good shape, and it's neat enough to give a party in."

Emma straightened in surprise, wiping her hands on her apron. "Farley's no housekeeper. Are you sure you were in the right place?"

"There's something afoot," Ben said.

"What could it be? Did he drop any hints?" Emma asked.

"Not a one, far as I could tell." Ben thought a moment, then added, "He's due back in five days. Maybe then he'll let us in on his secret."

Lady scratched at the back door, and Megan hurried to open it to let her out. The day gleamed with sunlight, and Megan raced into it with Lady, feeling a part of the golden warmth. What a glorious season it had been so far. As much as she missed her family, Megan knew she couldn't have wanted kinder or more generous people than Emma and Ben to have taken her into their home. Gypsy or no gypsy, it seemed the time for Megan to have some good luck had finally arrived. With Lady at her heels, Megan ran around and around the yard. Her arms became wings as she ran in wider and wider cir-

**51**

cles, kicking up puffs of dust, swooping and twirling and laughing as Lady tried to keep up.

Suddenly Lady dashed against her legs, and Megan tripped over her and fell sprawling on the ground. Lady was zigzagging back and forth in front of Megan, barking furiously.

Brushing dust from the front of her dress, Megan struggled to her knees to see what had caused Lady to go into such a frenzy. Coiled next to an overturned tub, half-hidden in its shade, was a large rattlesnake.

Megan stared in terror at the wide-stretched mouth with its threatening fangs and darting, quivering tongue. The snake's head swayed from side to side, following Lady's every movement.

Megan screamed and scrambled to her feet. "Look out, Lady!" she yelled. "Get back! Get away!"

For just an instant Lady turned her head toward Megan, as though to make sure that she was safely out of harm's way, and during that brief moment the rattlesnake struck.

# 6

THE DOOR BANGED as Ben rushed from the house. He scooped up Megan and carried her well out of the rattle-snake's range. Emma, puffing and gasping, one hand pressed against her abdomen, thrust a hoe into Ben's hand.

Too shocked to move, Megan watched Ben slam down the hoe on the snake. Its long thick body twitched and undulated, and its tail of rattles rose and slapped the ground even after it was dead.

Lady walked slowly to Megan and lay down at her feet, looking up at her with a puzzled expression. Megan dropped to wrap her arms around Lady, who licked her cheek. "Do something for her!" Megan cried. "Help her!"

"There's nothing we can do," Emma said. Her words ended in a sob, and Megan burrowed her face into Lady's fur.

"It's my fault!" Megan wailed. "I called to her. She turned to look at me."

"It's no one's fault," Ben said.

"I wasn't watching. I wasn't thinking. She tried to protect me."

Ben put a hand on Megan's shoulder. "Don't blame yourself. It's rare to find a snake that large in the open, where people are working. Matter of fact, it's late in the year for a snake to be out. By this time they're all usually in hibernation, but we've been without rain for a long time, and this dry spell—"

His voice broke, and he knelt beside Megan to stroke Lady's head.

The dog was quiet now, shivering as the poison spread through her body. Megan held her tightly. "Oh, Lady, Lady," Megan sobbed. "Please don't die!" Lady nestled against her, as though she trusted Megan to take care of her.

Megan squeezed her eyes tightly shut but gasped in horror as she saw through the blackness the grinning face of the old gypsy woman. "Bad luck," the gypsy cackled. "Bad penny."

"No, no!" Megan moaned.

"Megan." Ben's voice was soft. "Get up, Megan."

She raised her head. "But Lady—"

"It's over," he said. He gently unwound Megan's arms from around Lady and pulled her to her feet. "Why don't you wash your face and go into the house with Emma? I'll take care of Lady."

"I want to stay with her."

"There are things that you'll need to do."

"But I—"

"Someone will have to feed Lady's pups."

Megan gasped. "The pups! I forgot about them! What will happen to them without their mother?"

Emma took Megan around by the back door to wash her face. While Megan scrubbed away the tears and dust with cold water and a lump of lye soap, Emma said, "They'll take cow's milk with a bit of sugar in it. We'll tear some clean rags into strips, dip them into the milk, and wind them into nipples the pups can suck from."

Megan glanced back toward the spot where Lady lay as Emma shepherded her into the house, but she couldn't see around Emma. As they entered the house the pups were yipping and whining. Their tails waggled in eagerness as they spotted Megan, who sat on the floor by the box. "I'm sorry," Megan murmured.

"It wasn't your fault," Emma told her. She carefully put down a bowl of milk on the floor next to Megan and handed her a narrow strip of unbleached cotton cloth. Kneeling beside Megan, Emma showed her how to tightly twist the cloth strips before dipping them into the milk.

Emma picked up Moby and thrust a cloth nipple into his mouth. Moby fought against it, loudly complaining, until he tasted the sugared milk that dripped onto his chin. Then he tentatively allowed Emma to dip the cloth and poke it into his mouth again. This time he sucked noisily at it.

Megan chose Peg, the littlest, and followed Emma's lead. "They took the milk nicely," Emma said as they finished, although by the time Megan had fed Peg and Patches, her dress was splattered with milk. Clumsily, with Megan helping her, Emma climbed to her feet. "We know how often Lady fed her pups, and we can keep the same schedule."

"I'll do it," Megan said. "It's too hard for you, and it's my—my responsibility."

Heartbroken, she gazed up at Emma, who wrapped her arms around Megan, hugging her close. "Oh, Megan!" Emma's voice trembled. "I miss Lady, too, but dear little girl, I'm so very, very thankful that it wasn't *you!*"

"Lady died because of me," Megan whispered. "I brought the bad luck."

"No, you didn't!" Emma was emphatic. "Sorrow is a part of everyone's life. We expect it and learn to live with it. I don't want you blaming yourself for what happened. You mustn't think for a moment that you were the cause of the bad luck. That's not true!"

But Megan could still see the gypsy's face and hear the gypsy's bad-luck curse. Lady would not have died if she hadn't been protecting Megan. Megan woke that night hearing Emma's muffled tears, and she curled into a small, tight ball of misery. First her family had been split apart; now poor Lady was gone forever. Megan couldn't even bear to imagine what sorrow she would bring next to the ones she loved.

In the morning, Megan had no time to think about what might take place, busy as she was with tasks that had to be done no matter what else happened.

The pups took the sugared milk greedily each time it was offered, and by the third day Megan stopped worrying about them, assured that they'd continue to grow stronger and healthier.

It was just after she'd finished feeding them their evening meal that she and Emma, who was browning sugar in the iron skillet to make a caramelized sauce for custard, heard a horse's hoofbeats on the road.

Megan opened the door to see not Mr. Haskill but a lean, deeply tanned man who swung down from his horse to talk to Ben. The two men walked toward the barn, the stranger holding his horse's bridle, and Megan popped back inside the house, quietly shutting the door. "It's not Mr. Haskill. It's someone else," she said.

Emma looked up from her work. "Who?"

**56**

"I don't know. A man alone who came on horseback."

"In any case, we'll have a guest for supper," Emma said, her glance darting critically about the room. "It's a good thing there's plenty of side meat. And wasn't it lucky I picked today to make a custard? Put an extra plate on the table, and oh—that rug by the fireplace—does it need shaking out?" As she spoke, Emma briskly stirred the contents of the skillet.

"The rug looks fine to me," Megan said, smiling at the way Emma's eyes were shining at the prospect of having a visitor.

Within a few minutes Ben led the man into the house, to be greeted by Emma, who had changed to a fresh apron, and Megan, whose scalp still tingled from having her hair quickly brushed.

"This is Mr. Thomas Cartwright," Ben said. "I've invited him to stay the night with us."

"Ma'am," Mr. Cartwright said, quickly pulling off his wide-brimmed felt hat to expose a roughly cut shock of dark hair. He smiled at Megan, too.

"You'll share our supper, Mr. Cartwright?" Emma said.

"With pleasure." Mr. Cartwright leaned his bulging saddlebags against the wall. He eyed the table so eagerly that Megan knew he must be hungry.

"Then sit right down," Emma said. "Megan and I will dish up the meal right away."

"We're having custard for dessert," Megan told Mr. Cartwright, and he smiled so broadly that a dimple flickered in his right cheek.

"My favorite," he said, "and it's been at least two years since I've eaten any."

Emma and Megan put the bowls of mashed squash and sliced cooked potatoes—both dotted with butter made from Rosie's milk—in the center of the table, and

**57**

Ben brought the platter of fried meat. There was bread and more butter, and Megan could smell real coffee—instead of the usual chicory—being brewed in honor of the visitor.

They bowed their heads as Ben said grace, and the bowls were passed first to Mr. Cartwright, who—without waiting for any encouragement, Megan noticed—scooped liberal portions onto his plate and ate with obvious enjoyment.

But Megan was more curious than hungry. "Are you a Kansas farmer, too, Mr. Cartwright?" she asked.

He wiped his lips with his napkin and laid it back on his lap before he answered. "No," he said. "I'm employed by the United States Department of the Interior."

Megan had no idea what that meant, but Emma said, "Oh, my!" and looked impressed.

"Surveying the land?" Ben asked.

"In a way," Mr. Cartwright said. "I was hired to travel with a United States Army western survey crew and make detailed sketches of the countryside."

"You're an artist? A real one?" Megan dropped her fork on the table and stared. She'd seen a few paintings in public buildings, even one in the entrance hall of the Children's Aid Society. She'd been amazed when Mike told her there were homes uptown with large, gold-framed paintings hanging right in their living rooms. But she'd never seen a painter before.

"Yes, I'm an artist. That's my business." The dimple in his cheek came back as he said, "I'm on my way home from a California-to-Oregon branch survey with many of my drawings and sketches."

"All the way to California!" Emma said. "What is it like out there?"

"I can best show you through my sketches," Mr. Cartwright said. "Would you like to see them after we've finished supper?"

"*I* would!" Megan said. Ben and Emma eagerly agreed.

"I've heard of the artists of the western surveys," Ben said. "I'd like to know more about the kind of work you do."

The men began talking about the expeditions: some sent to map and explore, some to define boundaries, and some to survey land for proposed rail lines.

"I've worked with some notable artists," Mr. Cartwright said. "Solomon Carvalho and Richard Kern. Unfortunately Kern was killed during a Paiute Indian attack in Utah."

Megan's question came out in a whisper. "Were you there when Mr. Kern was killed?"

"Yes," he said. "I was with the expedition."

She knew the expression on her face must show the horror she felt, because he added, "The Indians don't understand our taking over their land, and they certainly don't like it. They're afraid, and sometimes they're angry when we slaughter their food supply."

"Buffalo," Ben said.

"That's right." Mr. Cartwright turned back to Megan. "I've been able to make many friends among the Indians, and along with my watercolors and sketches of the countryside, I've done some portraits of the Indians."

"Do you have those with you, too? Could we see them?" Megan asked.

"I have a few. Whatever I've brought with me, I'll be glad to show you."

Emma had brought the custard to the table and spooned it into bowls. Megan gulped her portion without tasting it and could hardly wait until the adults had finished eating. A real artist! And he was going to show them the

**59**

sketches and paintings he'd made! Wouldn't she have something grand to tell Mike!

After the dishes had been done, Ben brought in the oil lamps from the bedrooms so that in addition to the glow from the fire there would be as much light as possible in the room. One at a time Mr. Cartwright unrolled the paintings he had pulled from his saddlebags. At the sight of the towering mountains, crashing surf, and churning, foaming rivers, Megan could only gasp in amazement.

"These places are real?"

"I drew what I saw with my own eyes."

Megan smoothed down the curled edges of the pencil sketch in front of her, admiring the way Mr. Cartwright had drawn long shadows beside the rocks and pines. "I would love to see these places someday."

"Someday you will," he said seriously. "It won't be long before the railroads will cross the West, and people won't think anything at all of traveling all the way from the Atlantic Ocean to the Pacific." He nodded importantly. "Why, I even predict that someday, probably when you are grown, Megan, travelers will be able to accomplish this feat within two weeks."

Emma laughed aloud, and Ben slowly shook his head, a grin appearing on his face. "I think you're asking us to believe in the impossible, Mr. Cartwright," he said.

Megan tried to picture in her mind the faraway places in Mr. Cartwright's drawings. What did it matter how long it would take to get to them? The important part was to see them, and someday she would.

Mr. Cartwright pulled another roll of drawings from his saddlebags and carefully untied the cord. "Here are some of my sketches of Indians," he said as he laid the drawings on the table.

Megan was even more interested in these than in the

beautiful scenes of mountain country. She smiled at a sketch of an Indian baby peering with bright eyes from the pack on his mother's back. There was an old man—"a tribal chieftain," Mr. Cartwright explained—whose face was a mass of deep, squiggly wrinkles. And there was a girl with black eyes who made Megan think of the Indian girl she had seen on the road.

Megan was surprised when Mr. Cartwright suddenly lifted her chin with one finger and studied her face. "I would like to sketch you," he said. "Would you sit very still by the fireplace where the light can shine on your hair? It will be just a sketch, so it won't take long."

Megan nodded, and Emma beamed with pleasure. "See, Megan," she said. "Mr. Cartwright thinks you are beautiful, too."

"Yes," Mr. Cartwright said. "Megan's a lovely young lady, but I see something more than just beauty. It's the special look in her eyes I want to capture."

"What look?" Megan asked, blushing because everyone was studying her.

"I'm not sure," he answered. "I think I see a little sorrow, a little happiness, and some memories you've kept secret from all but yourself."

Emma's eyes widened and she nervously smoothed down her apron. "Would you like Megan to change to another dress?" Emma asked. "She has a lovely dark red one. Should I braid her hair?"

"I want to sketch Megan exactly the way she is now." Mr. Cartwright pulled some pencils from his pack and attached a small sheet of paper to a flat, smooth board. He stationed Megan on a footstool near the hearth and tilted her head a little to the left so that a long strand of her dark hair fell over one shoulder. "Don't move," he said and went back to his chair.

**61**

With Emma standing behind him murmuring, "Oh, yes! Oh, that's very like her!" and Ben leaning sideways now and then to sneak glances at the sketch, Mr. Cartwright worked with quick, sure strokes. In about fifteen minutes he said, "If you don't mind holding the pose a while longer, Megan, we'll have a sketch for you and one for me."

"I don't mind," she said, trying not to move her head. Mr. Cartwright took the sketch off the board and handed it to an admiring Emma, who cooed and clucked over it. He attached another sheet and set to work again.

When he had finished, he put both sketches on the table and beckoned to Megan. "I'll give you your choice," he said.

Megan stared at the sketches, her heart beating faster. She had seen herself in mirrors or reflected in window glass, but now she was looking at a different Megan. The same pointed chin, the same dark, straight hair, but eyes that held their own story. In those eyes she could see some of Da's mischief, some of Ma's smile, and her own unshed tears. "That girl is really me," she whispered in awe.

"Megan seems a little solemn in your drawings, but they're beautiful!" Emma exclaimed. Megan could feel Emma's excitement tingle through her own body as Emma wrapped an arm around her shoulders. "What a wonderful honor to have an artist draw your picture!"

Megan was amazed at the sketches. They showed more about her than she wanted people to see, even more than she wanted to see herself. How had Mr. Cartwright known what she was like inside?

"What will you do with the sketch I give you?" Mr. Cartwright asked.

Megan thought for a moment. "I'll put it away carefully where it can't be harmed. It will be my treasure."

---

"If it's put away, you can't see it and enjoy it," Emma said. "Ben can make a frame for it."

"Which one do you choose?" Mr. Cartwright asked.

Megan couldn't decide. She closed her eyes and pointed to one of the sketches. "This one."

"It's yours," Mr. Cartwright said. He signed the bottom of the sheet of paper with a flourish and began to pack his materials and roll up his sketches and paintings.

"What will you do with the other sketch of me?" Megan asked him.

"I'm not sure," he said. "Maybe someday I'll use it as the basis of a painting. Maybe I'll frame it as it is and include it in a showing of my sketches on the trail. Maybe I'll just enjoy looking at it." He grinned and added, "If I manage to become a famous artist, you might become famous yourself. The sketch may hang in a museum, and the people who look at it will ask, 'Who is this mystery girl?' And no one will know until you come forward to tell them."

"There's an easier solution to the problem," Megan said. "Just write my name on the back of the paper."

Mr. Cartwright looked so startled that Ben laughed. "Megan takes a practical approach to life," Ben said. He turned to Megan. "Mr. Cartwright has a long way to travel tomorrow, so I think we should let him get his rest tonight," he said.

Emma made a pallet on the floor near the fireplace for their visitor. Megan went to her own room, carrying her oil lamp in one hand and the sketch Mr. Cartwright had made of her in the other. With her door closed, she laid the sketch on the bed and examined it. She liked the way he had drawn her to be a little like Ma, a little like Da. As for the secrets, only Mr. Cartwright and she had seen them, so they were still her own.

**63**

She tightly rolled the sketch again and placed it in the bottom of the chest, where it would be safe until Ben made a frame for it.

In the morning, after a hearty breakfast of boiled eggs and wheat bread with wild plum jam, Mr. Cartwright said his farewells and rode away toward the east. Megan washed the dishes, fed the pups again, and went out to the barn to lend a hand to Ben.

She had just finished forking great loads of clean hay into the stalls when she heard a loud "Halloo" and the rattle and creak of a wagon. She raced to the front of the house, pulling wisps of hay from her tousled hair and trying to brush the dust from her skirt. This time it had to be Mr. Haskill.

It was, but someone was with him. Megan stopped short, suddenly shy as a woman in a dark blue coat stared at her from the seat of the wagon. The woman was tall and thin, with deep-set eyes shaded by the ostrich plumes on her wide-brimmed hat. She was not a young woman and not very pretty; her nose was pinched and narrow, and her heavy eyebrows were darker than her hair. Megan, remembering her manners, tried to smile, but the woman looked away from her, studying the Browders' house.

Ben came up behind Megan and took the horse's bridle. "Farley!" he said. "Come in! Come in!" He turned to the woman, unable to conceal his surprise.

Farley jumped from the wagon and hurried to help the woman climb down. "I'd like you to meet my wife, Ada Blackwell—uh, that is, Ada Haskill. Ada, this is Ben Browder and his daughter, Megan."

"Well, well. I'm pleased as punch for you, Farley," Ben stammered. "It's good to meet you, ma'am. Emma will be so happy to have a woman as a close neighbor."

The woman answered with a nod, then turned toward the front door, which Emma had just flung open.

"Farley!" Emma shouted, then saw the woman. Her mouth opened and she blinked a couple of times before she was able to smile a welcome.

"Farley's brought home a wife!" Ben called to Emma. "This is Ada. Ada, I'd like you to meet my wife, Emma."

Emma ran awkwardly toward Ada, her arms spread wide in welcome. "I'm so happy to meet you," she said. "I'm so happy for Farley!"

Ada accepted Emma's hug stiffly and with surprise. "How do you do?" she said formally. Her speech sounded a little strange, almost foreign, to Megan.

"You must stay for dinner," Emma said. "Please—come inside. I know you're tired from your long ride. Did you come from St. Joseph? Have you seen Farley's—your— home yet? Have you had a chance to unpack?"

Ben smiled. "Emma, let Ada sit down before you start in asking questions." As the women walked toward the house, Ben began to unhitch Farley's horse. "We'll stable this fellow in the barn with some feed," he said to Farley, "and you can tell me how you met your wife."

Megan looked from the women to the men, not sure which way to go. She decided to follow Emma. This was a very interesting turn of events, and she was sure that Emma would be able to find out more of the details than Ben ever would.

By the time Megan arrived inside the house, Mrs. Haskill had taken off her coat and was removing her hat, placing it on a small table near the window. Jet beads on the long hatpins winked and gleamed in the sunlight. Megan touched a finger to the silver-blue plumes. "Your hat is beautiful!" she murmured.

"Thank you," Mrs. Haskill said. Under her heavy brows she gave Megan a curious look.

"You're dressed like the ladies in New York City," Megan said. "Do you come from there?"

"No, I do not," Mrs. Haskill said. "I am from England. I came to the United States and resided for a short while in Boston with distant cousins."

Emma came forward with a cup of tea. "Here," she said. "I'm sure you need this." As Mrs. Haskill accepted the cup, Emma sat in a chair facing her. "Tell me how you came to meet Farley," she said. "He's never been to Boston."

Mrs. Haskill took a long sip of the tea and gave a little shudder. "This is not *English* tea," she said.

"Why, no," Emma answered. "It's made from dried herbs and leaves. My good friend Nelda made the mixture for me. It has a pleasing flavor, don't you think?"

Mrs. Haskill didn't answer. She took another sip of tea and stared into the cup as though she were thinking very hard. Finally she raised her head and looked directly at Emma. "My marriage with Mr. Haskill was arranged," she said. "We corresponded with each other, and I agreed to travel to St. Joseph to meet him. Our meeting seemed pleasurable to both of us, so we were married two days ago."

"Oh." Emma looked embarrassed. "How nice for both of you."

Mrs. Haskill drained the cup of tea and shrugged. "An impoverished woman, without close kin to care for her, has little choice but to marry. The situation in my cousins' home had become disagreeable, so I decided to take this opportunity to live in the West." Her nostrils seemed to become even more pinched as she added, "However, I must say that I expected the western part of this country to be quite different from the way I found it. This Kansas territory is hardly an attractive place in which to live."

"You don't see beauty in the prairie?" Megan was so astonished that she interrupted without thinking. "Of course, right now the grass is turning brown, but Emma says that in the spring the hills will be green and there will be wildflowers."

Mrs. Haskill looked at her sharply, then turned to Emma. "Your daughter doesn't favor you," she said. "Your eyes are brown, as are your husband's, and the girl's eyes are blue. And her speech. If I didn't know better, I'd think—"

She broke off, and Emma said, "Oh, Megan is our adopted child. We chose her."

"I'm from New York City," Megan said. "My name is Megan Eileen Kelly." Trying to put Mrs. Haskill more at ease, she smiled and added, "And don't feel badly about being impoverished. I was impoverished, too."

Mrs. Haskill turned to Emma with bewilderment and said, "I'm sure your intentions were excellent, but I fail to understand how you could possibly take into your home a child who is—who is shanty Irish!"

# 7

MEGAN GASPED, UNABLE to believe her ears. The color rose in Emma's cheeks, and her eyes sparked as shock gave way to anger. Deliberately she smoothed her apron over her knees, tilted her chin a little higher, and said firmly, "Mrs. Haskill, I'm sure you're so exhausted from the long ride that you don't know what you're saying."

Mrs. Haskill looked puzzled as she tried to explain, speaking as though Megan weren't there. "But my dear Mrs. Browder, I do know what I'm saying. It's common knowledge that the Irish are dull-witted and lazy and therefore never able to rise above the laboring class."

"There's not one word of truth in that statement!" Emma said.

Megan's face burned hot with anger, and she gripped the seat of her chair, trying to keep from speaking the words she was thinking.

Mrs. Haskill appeared flustered. One hand crept to her cheeks, which were pink with embarrassment. When she spoke, her tone was conciliatory, and her words came slowly, as though she believed she could persuade Emma to listen to reason. "You are obviously not as knowledge-able about the Irish as the English are, since we have had closer dealings with them."

Megan knew about those "closer dealings." She well remembered Da's stories about the British armies that swept across Ireland, burning homes and tearing the roofs from churches. No allegiance was allowed except to the British Crown, and property was stolen from landowners and given to subjects loyal to England. Those Irish who emigrated to England or the United States, trying to keep from starving, found that laboring jobs were the only ones given to them—if jobs were offered at all.

"I am not alone in my beliefs," Mrs. Haskill continued. "In Boston it is quite usual to see, in the windows of shops and small businesses, Help Wanted advertisements that specify 'No Irish need apply.'" She leaned back in her chair and folded her hands in her lap as though the discussion had come to a satisfactory conclusion.

But Emma hadn't finished. "It's a pity that in Boston there are so many small-minded, mealymouthed people who can't see beyond the ends of their turned-up noses! I hope that living in Kansas with people who know how to value each other will broaden your education, Mrs. Haskill." Emma's eyes bored into the other woman's as she leaned forward and snapped, "And perhaps greatly improve your manners!"

Mrs. Haskill gasped, and her teacup rattled so hard in its saucer that she had to put it on the table.

The door flew open. Ben and Mr. Haskill stomped the dust from their feet on the front stoop and stepped into the room.

"Well, well," Ben said, beaming at the two women. "You should be pretty well acquainted by now. Emma, I told Ada and Farley that you'd be excited about having another woman as a close neighbor." Ben turned to Mr. Haskill. "We'll see if Emma can make us a little something special for dinner to celebrate."

Emma sat staring straight ahead with her back stiff and her hands so tightly folded her knuckles were white. She didn't repeat the invitation.

"I—I'm sure that Emma would—" Ben blundered on, but Mrs. Haskill interrupted him. Trembling, she rose to her feet.

"No, thank you," she said. "I wish to become acquainted with my new home as soon as possible."

"But we—" Mr. Haskill began.

Ignoring her husband, Mrs. Haskill glanced around the room and sighed. "Living in this primitive fashion is going to be quite a change for me."

Emma's eyes narrowed with concern as she asked Mr. Haskill, "Farley, have you told Ada anything about your home?"

Mr. Haskill looked uncomfortable. "I—I've never had the words to describe things easily," he stammered. "Anyhow, I figured there'd be things she'd want to do to fix it up her own way." He threw a panic-stricken glance at Ben. "I gave it a good cleaning afore I left. Did it look all right to you?"

"It looked fine," Ben said. "I told Emma I couldn't get over how well you'd cleaned it."

Mr. Haskill let out a long sigh of relief. Ben glanced from Emma to Mrs. Haskill, and Megan could see that he was confused by the tension in the air.

"Emma," he said, "we can fix up a basket of things for Ada to take to her new home. Put in a loaf or two of the bread you baked this morning, and some of your plum jam."

Without a word Emma walked to the kitchen table,

opened the nearby cupboard, and began to put things into a woven reed basket.

"Ada, you'll love Emma's wild plum jam," Ben continued. "I'm sure she'll teach you to make your own, come summer when the fruit is ripe."

The pups began to yip and whine, and Mrs. Haskill glanced toward their box, wrinkling her nose in distaste. She turned to Ben, and her voice was cold. "I know how to make jam, thank you. I am well versed in all the disciplines needed to operate a household."

Ben rubbed his chin before he answered, and Megan could see that he was sizing up Mrs. Haskill. But he said amiably, "Neighbors are a real necessity out here where families are spaced so far apart. We're glad to welcome you to the territory, and if you need or want for anything, we're here to help you out. Farley's always been a good neighbor to us, and we're mighty thankful to have him nearby."

Mr. Haskill clapped a hand on Ben's shoulder, mumbling his own thanks, but Mrs. Haskill gave an imperious nod. She gracefully put on her coat, looked around the room for a mirror, and finding none, impatiently pinned on her elegant hat. "As soon as I've unpacked my china, Mr. Haskill and I will invite you to dine," she said.

Ben blinked with surprise. Emma strode to where Mrs. Haskill was standing and shoved a napkin-covered basket at her. Mrs. Haskill had no choice but to grab the handle before the basket fell on her toes.

"Thank you," Mrs. Haskill said formally.

"You're welcome." Emma's words were equally cool.

Ben and Mr. Haskill left to hitch the horses, and Mrs. Haskill followed. Emma hesitated, obviously torn between following the basic rules of courtesy and giving in to her feelings. Firmly she shut the door and wrapped her arms around Megan.

"It's the Irish in you that makes you so special and wonderful," she murmured against Megan's hair. "Pay no attention to what that dreadful woman said!"

Megan hugged her back, having trouble getting her arms about Emma's waist, which seemed to be growing thicker each day. "I've heard things like that before," Megan reassured her. "There were some in New York City who had no use for the Irish or for that matter anyone different from themselves. Ma told us to feel sorry for them because they were not only ignorant but wanted to stay that way."

Emma smiled. "A good description of Ada Haskill."

"I don't like her," Megan said.

"Neither do I. But then who would?" Emma filled the kettle from the jar that held fresh water brought from the well that morning and hung it on one of the arms at the side of the fireplace, swinging it over the fire to heat up. "It's perfectly clear why she couldn't find a husband in Boston and had to come west to marry Farley."

"Poor Mr. Haskill," Megan said. She peeked through the window and watched Mrs. Haskill struggle with her skirts as she climbed to the seat of the wagon.

"Poor Mr. Haskill should have had his head examined before marrying that woman!" With a clatter Emma slammed a stack of tin plates onto the table.

"She tries to be very grand," Megan said, "and she thinks that Mr. Haskill's house is like yours. I wonder what she'll do when she finds that she'll be living underground."

Megan and Emma looked at each other with such mischief that they burst into laughter. At that moment Ben came into the house. He stared at them in amazement, which made them laugh all the harder.

"There must be something here I don't understand," he said, which caused Emma to whoop.

72

She leaned against the table, wiping her eyes with the hem of her apron. "Ada Haskill—" she began, but couldn't stop laughing.

Ben rubbed his chin again and turned to Megan. "I didn't see anything about the woman that would cause the two of you so much merriment. Was it her hat?"

This set off another outburst, until finally Emma was able to say, "It's the idea of a woman like that having to live in a dugout."

Ben didn't smile. He shook his head and said seriously, "Emma, we must set a good example for Megan. It's not right to laugh at someone's misfortune. We began our work here by living in a dugout, and you know the many hardships it caused you."

Emma wiped her eyes again and glanced at Megan, whose stomach ached from laughing so hard. "Ben is right," Emma said. "This should be a happy day for Farley, and I'm afraid it's going to be unhappy for both himself and Ada. I shouldn't have laughed."

"I'm sorry, too," Megan said to Ben.

"Oh, Ben," Emma said, "it wasn't what it seemed. The laughter helped us to keep from being angry."

"Angry? Just because the woman seemed somewhat . . . reserved?"

Emma told him all that Mrs. Haskill had said. For a moment the room was silent. Then Ben slammed a fist on the nearby table so hard that the lamp wobbled, and Megan reached to catch it before it fell. He turned and stomped out of the house, banging the door behind him.

"Don't look so worried," Emma reassured Megan. "Ben will work off his anger. Before long he'll begin to feel sorry for her. Then he'll try to think of how to make her feel welcome and accepted, so that she'll see how wrong she was and change her ways. By the time he comes to

**73**

dinner he'll be himself again." She smiled. "He's a good man, Megan."

Emma was right. By the time Megan had finished feeding the pups, Ben had come back. He sat down at the table and beamed at the steaming bowls of chicken and vegetables. When he bowed his head to say grace, he added an extra prayer for the well-being of Farley and Ada Haskill, then cheerfully set to filling the plates and passing them to Emma and Megan.

"Farley said that with the election just a few days away, feelings are high in St. Joe. There's talk of war if Lincoln is elected."

"Will you vote?" Megan asked him.

"I wish I could, but people in the territories don't have the vote," he answered. "Our elected representative to Congress can debate any issue, but even he doesn't have the right to vote on it."

They began to talk about Abraham Lincoln, who had come through eastern Kansas the year before on a speaking tour. Their words became a comfortable hum as Megan's thoughts drifted away. She thought again of Mrs. Haskill and pictured the woman's disapproving face. She'd try to feel sorry for her, as Ma had said, but Mrs. Haskill's words had hurt, and it was hard to feel anything but upset and angry. Suddenly, achingly, Megan was lonely for her mother.

It was evening, the animals cared for and stabled, and Megan and the Browders snug inside the house, when Mr. Haskill arrived on foot.

His tap on the door made Emma start, and she nearly dropped the lamp she was lighting.

Ben glanced at the rifles in their rack near the door and called, "Who's there?"

"It's me—Farley Haskill," the visitor answered.

"Not Ada again!" Emma breathed, but she put a fixed smile on her face and prepared to greet her neighbors.

Mr. Haskill entered alone, his head and neck tucked down inside the big collar of his coat as though he were trying to find a place to hide, and put the lantern he was carrying on the table.

Ben peered outside through the open door. "Where's Ada?"

"Home," Mr. Haskill mumbled. "She's sent me with a list of things she needs and wants me to borrow." He looked apologetically at Emma. "I tried to tell her that she can't take from the neighbors, that we'll have to ride to town for some of these things—those we can afford—but she—well, she insisted."

Megan could imagine how insistent Mrs. Haskill could be.

"Never mind, Farley," Emma said. She took the list from his hand. "Take off your coat and rest. Ben can pour some coffee for you—that is, ground hickory."

Mr. Haskill shrugged. "That's all I'm used to."

He looked so miserable that Megan felt sorry for him. She helped him take off his coat and hung it on the rack for him.

Emma read the list, nodding or shaking her head at each item. "I can give you some sugar. It's brown sugar, though, not the white Ada is used to."

"Brown's fine."

"And some sassafras. It's not on the list, but if she brews it in tea and drinks it good and hot it will help take away her headache. I don't have the headache powders she wants."

Mr. Haskill nodded.

For just a minute Emma closed her eyes and pursed

her lips as if she were trying to make a difficult decision. She gave a little sigh and said, "I do have one down pillow that I can lend her. My mother made it for me."

Mr. Haskill looked even more miserable than before. "It's not right to take it."

"What are neighbors for?" Emma said. "Of course you'll take it to Ada, if it will make her happy." She shook her head. "But I don't own a down quilt. I can give you a pieced quilt, though, that should be good and warm."

"I can't see that any of these things will make her happy," Mr. Haskill blurted out. "She thought we'd have a real house. I should have told her most folks out here start with a dugout. But Ada didn't know that. It's my fault. I guess it never occurred to me that it would matter so much to her. She's—well, she's been crying ever since I took her home."

Megan felt another brief pang of guilt for anticipating Mrs. Haskill's discomfort and laughing about it.

Emma patted Mr. Haskill's arm. "We'll help Ada to feel at home," she said. "Everything's strange to her now, but she'll come around."

"She wants a real house," Farley said. "She wants one built of lumber, and I can't afford to buy the logs yet."

"Tell you what, Farley," Ben said. "Why don't I help you cut sod bricks and build you a house up away from the river?"

Mr. Haskill brightened. "Do you think Ada would settle for a sod house?"

"It's better than a dugout," Ben said. "It would have more than one window. We could make two rooms in it, and Ada would feel like she had a real house."

"That's a kind offer. I can't thank you enough," Mr. Haskill said, and his eyes glistened in the lamplight.

"I'll put together as many of the things on this list as I've got on hand," Emma said, "and you stop worrying about Ada."

As Emma set to work, Megan sat on the footstool and studied Mr. Haskill. He took a long sip of his coffee, cradling the cup in his hands, and said, "I guess she's lonely for home."

"It's only natural for now," Ben said. "She'll get over it."

"I s'pose. I wonder how long it will take. Maybe a couple of weeks or so?"

"No," Megan told them. "Much longer than that."

Ben and Mr. Haskill looked at her with surprise. "The loneliness is inside," Megan said, pressing her hands against her stomach, "and sometimes you forget that it's there. But other times it makes a picture in your mind of the people you love—the people you left behind—and your stomach aches with the hurt of it all."

"Sounds like this is familiar to you," Mr. Haskill murmured, and Megan nodded.

"Even when we're laughing and talking sometimes the loneliness comes. I never know when it will happen."

"I think I understand," Mr. Haskill said.

"I think I do, too," Megan said. "About Mrs. Haskill, I mean."

The expression in Ben's eyes, as he looked at her, changed from concern to pride, and Megan smiled at him, no longer caring what Mrs. Haskill had said.

# 8

FOUR DAYS LATER Ben left before dawn, taking his wagon to the nearest town to get the iron strips on two of the wheels repaired. Soon after he had gone, Mr. Haskill arrived at the Browders' house, hallooing and shouting even before he reached the front door.

"It's Ada!" he cried in terror to Emma and Megan, who had rushed outside to meet him. "She's down sick with the fever!"

"It's too cold for the mosquitoes to be out, carrying the ague," Emma said, thinking aloud. "It's more likely that she's taken a chill. Does she have a cough?"

Mr. Haskill frowned. "Not exactly. More of a roughening of the voice."

"Good," Emma said. "I don't think it's serious. I'll give you something for her to drink that will help her sleep and some mustard seed to make a poultice, in case the roughness develops into a chest cough." She glanced toward the iron stove. "It won't take long to pluck a chicken and cook up a strong broth. I'll see that Ada gets it as soon as it's ready."

"I'll help," Megan offered.

"Thanks to you both," Mr. Haskill said. He looked greatly relieved, although there were such deep circles under his eyes that Megan wondered if he could be getting ill himself.

"For goodness' sakes, Farley, she'll be all right," Emma said. "We all take to our beds now and then. It's the way life is."

"It's because the house is damp," Farley said. "Ada said so."

"Damp? With a drought that has lasted more than a year?" Emma paused, and when she spoke again her voice was low and gentle. "Ada just isn't used to our ways yet, Farley. Be patient, and stop blaming yourself for everything she doesn't like. Soon she'll be blooming just like one of the prairie roses."

"You think so?"

"Why doubt it? She's strong and has a great deal more purpose to her than many women I've met. There's no reason she can't put those attributes to good use. Just you be patient."

Mr. Haskill looked considerably cheered as he left with the package Emma had prepared for him. The front door had no sooner shut behind him than Emma, snugly wrapped in one of Ben's heavy coats, was out the back door. Megan soon heard a loud squawking in the henhouse, and shortly Emma returned, an onion from the root cellar in one hand, a limp, gutted chicken in the other. Most of the large feathers had been plucked, but Megan set to work to pull the others, saving them carefully to add to Emma's hoard. As soon as the bag was full there'd be enough soft feathers to fill the small quilt Emma was making for the baby.

When Megan had finished her chore, Emma singed the

skin with a hot coal, washed the carcass in boiling water, and dropped it with the peeled and sliced onion into a large pot of water. She added some salt and two dried bay leaves and nodded with satisfaction. "This soup will be even better than medicine for her."

Megan noticed that Emma was moving more slowly than usual, stopping to rub her back with one hand. She knew what she could do to help. "I'll take the soup to Mrs. Haskill," she said.

Emma shook her head. "I don't want you exposed to her illness."

"I can get to the Haskills' house better and faster than you can, and I rarely come down ill. I was very good at nursing the others in my family."

Emma smiled. "I'm sure you were."

"I'd like to do something for Mrs. Haskill," Megan added.

"Because you feel guilty?" When Megan nodded in surprise, Emma said, "I do, too." She took the lid from the pot over the fire, stirred the contents, and replaced the lid with a satisfied smile. "Guilt is not the best reason for doing things, I must admit, but sometimes it does get the job done." She put her hands on Megan's shoulders. "We had reason to be angry at what she said, but the poor woman spoke out of ignorance."

Megan nodded. She hoped that Emma wouldn't begin to talk about forgiving. Ma had done that the day Megan came home in tears because two big girls had knocked her into the street and stolen the grocery money she was carrying. She hadn't been able to forgive those girls as her own stomach churned with hunger, and she didn't want to forgive Mrs. Haskill too quickly, not when her hard words about the Irish still burned in Megan's mind. Fortunately Emma gave Megan a quick kiss on the forehead and set about other household tasks.

Megan struggled into the heavy coat Emma had cut down for her and braved the chilly north winds in order to take care of chores in the barn.

When Emma called, Megan ran to get the pot of soup, well bundled to stay warm. She hurried down the road and across the plank bridge over the barely trickling river to the Haskill house.

Except for the underground root cellar, she had never been inside a dugout before. The one window let in very little light and, although the room was larger than she had imagined, the air was thick and stale. In a far corner of the room was a double bed, and in the bed lay Mrs. Haskill, her eyes and nose red—more from weeping than from chilblains, Megan decided.

Mr. Haskill fumbled with the soup pot as he took it from Megan, almost dropping it. "You have your farm chores to do, Mr. Haskill," she said. "I'll take good care of your wife."

He looked so relieved that it was hard for Megan not to smile as he rushed from the room. She spooned some of the steaming, fragrant soup into a bowl and carried it to Mrs. Haskill.

"I don't feel like eating," Mrs. Haskill said and turned her face to the hard-packed dirt wall. Her dark hair clung in damp strings to her face, and there were deep shadows under her eyes.

In spite of her dislike, Megan felt a pang of pity for the woman. "You'll feel better for having something this good in your stomach," she said. She put down the bowl and pulled a ladder-back chair next to the bed. Before Mrs. Haskill realized what was happening, Megan had hoisted her to a sitting position and plumped up Emma's down pillow behind her, adding an extra one, tightly stuffed with chicken feathers, to support her shoulders.

Megan had often helped to make Da comfortable in this same way during his illness. She thought of his gentle smile and the love in his eyes as she had carefully brought each spoonful of soup to his lips.

Megan would have done anything for Da because she loved him, but there was no way in the world that she could love Mrs. Haskill. Still, the woman needed caring for, and Megan was determined to do a good job of it.

"Now," Megan said firmly as she seated herself and picked up the bowl and spoon, "you'll have some of this fine soup that Emma Browder made for you."

She filled the spoon and held it out. Obediently Mrs. Haskill opened her mouth and swallowed the soup. By the third spoonful, a little color began to come into her cheeks. When the spoon scraped the bottom of the bowl, Megan asked, "Do you want more?"

Mrs. Haskill rubbed her nose with a damp cotton handkerchief and sniffed. "Perhaps a little more, although it's lacking a bit in flavor. I don't suppose Mrs. Browder thought of seasoning the broth with celery tops."

"At this time of the year there is no celery to be had," Megan answered. She filled the bowl again and spoon-fed Mrs. Haskill, who just lay there and allowed herself to be fed.

"When you plant your vegetable garden in the spring," Megan said, "maybe you could plant some celery seed in it. We're going to plant cucumbers, and Emma promised to show me how to make pickles."

Mrs. Haskill shuddered. She pushed the empty bowl away and dabbed at her lips with the handkerchief.

Megan tried to think of something to cheer her up. "Did Mr. Haskill tell you that he and Mr. Browder are going to build you a new house?" she asked.

Mrs. Haskill's eyes flashed, and she snapped, "A house built of earth!"

"What kind of house did you live in when you were in Boston?"

"A lovely brick house!"

"Well then," Megan said, "you lived in an earth house. That's what bricks are made of. I know, because my father helped to build brick houses."

"It's not the same," Mrs. Haskill said and sighed. "I don't expect anyone to understand." She shivered. "This dreadful house is so dark and cold."

Megan nodded. "Especially over here in the corner. Hop up, and we'll move the bed closer to the stove."

Mrs. Haskill tugged the quilt up to her neck. "Why, I'll do no such thing!" she complained. "Why should I let a little slip of a girl order me about?"

"Very well. Then I'll just pull my chair closer to the stove," Megan said. She did so and let out a long, contented sigh. If Mike had been there, he would have groaned and told her she was overdoing it, but Megan could think of no reasonable way to deal with Mrs. Haskill. The easiest solution would be to let her remain cold, but Megan had taken on Mrs. Haskill as a responsibility, and she was determined to help the poor woman, whether she wanted help or not. "Ah, yes," Megan said loudly. "It's much more comfortable over here."

Mrs. Haskill watched Megan for only a few moments before she said, "I suppose that together we could manage to move the bed." She slipped from under the quilt, her long flannel gown flapping around her legs, and tugged at the head of the bed. With Megan pulling at the foot, they slid the bed across the hard-packed floor until it was near the stove.

Megan moved the soup to the back of the small stove to stay warm. Then she took some dried cow chips from the basket, dropped them onto the coals, and replaced the heavy iron lid.

**83**

Mrs. Haskill shuddered, closing her eyes, and Megan saw a tear run down her cheek. "Would you like some of the medicine to help you sleep?" she asked.

"No," Mrs. Haskill snapped. "I'm not sleepy."

"Would you like me to tell you a story?" Emma was still delighted each time Megan told her one of the Irish legends that had been Da's favorites.

"I am not in the mood for childish stories."

"How about one of Mr. Aesop's fables? They each have a lesson to think about, although that's the best I can say for them."

"No!"

Megan frantically groped for a topic of conversation. There must be something they could talk about. "Why don't you tell me about yourself?" Megan asked.

Mrs. Haskill frowned. "You couldn't possibly understand, and even if you did, it would be of no interest to you." She rolled her head back and forth on the pillow. "I was sure that Mrs. Browder would come. Why did she send a child in her place?"

"I asked to come," Megan answered. "I wanted to help you. I also wanted to keep Emma—Mrs. Browder—from having to make the long walk. She's uncomfortable and awkward with the child she's carrying." Megan sat upright as a thought occurred to her. "Sure, it's grand that you're so close at hand! She plans to have another woman with her when the baby is born, but the woman lives far off. I've worried what would happen if there's snow and the travel is slow. But now that you're here, everything will be fine."

"You surely don't expect me to help deliver Mrs. Browder's child!" Mrs. Haskill's words ended in a squeak of horror.

Megan was puzzled. "I thought you'd want to help."

"Certainly not! That's not a proper task for a lady, although I can't expect you to understand that."

"I understand that if something needs to be done, then whoever is able should do it."

"We should not be having this conversation," Mrs. Haskill said. "A woman's—umm—delicate condition is not a proper topic for a lady to discuss."

"If we don't discuss it, then how will either of us know what the other is thinking about it?"

Mrs. Haskill punched at her pillow. "There is no need to continue this conversation. Mrs. Browder will have to call in a doctor or a midwife, as any sensible woman should."

"The doctor is in town—a very long ride away—and as for—"

"Ohhh! I hate this place!" Mrs. Haskill cried out. Her lower lip trembled as she turned to Megan. "Bring me my medicine. I believe I will sleep, after all. And then see if you can tidy this room. Even you should be able to do that task."

Megan clamped her teeth together as she obeyed Mrs. Haskill's orders. The woman was insulting and unkind. Worst of all, she'd said she wouldn't help Emma, who had been so good to her.

Mrs. Haskill snatched the bottle and spoon from Megan and attempted to pour out a dose of medicine. Fearing that some might spill on Emma's treasured down pillow, Megan reached out to steady Mrs. Haskill's hand, and a few drops of the liquid dropped onto the front of Mrs. Haskill's gown.

"You clumsy girl!" Mrs. Haskill cried. "Bring me a damp cloth. See if you can get the spots out of my gown!"

"I'm sorry," Megan said. She poured a few drops of

water from the kettle onto a clean cloth that lay on the table. "I thought you'd spill it on the pillow," she explained. "Mrs. Browder's mother made that pillow just for her. It's very special."

"It doesn't look that special. It's covered in a rather poor-quality cotton fabric. The down pillow I had in Boston had a linen pillowcase." Mrs. Haskill swallowed the medicine and handed the bottle and spoon to Megan. She rubbed at the spots on her gown, then tossed the cloth to the floor and sank back against the pillow with a sigh.

Megan picked up the broom that stood in the corner, but Mrs. Haskill said, "Put that back. It will only stir up the dust and make me cough."

Mrs. Haskill was silent for a few moments, and Megan asked, "What would you like me to do?"

Mrs. Haskill sighed again. "This is what I meant about the Irish. Can't you think for yourself?"

Megan gripped the edge of the table. She wanted to storm out of this place and never set eyes on the woman again, but she had promised to help, and she would keep her promise. With trembling hands she poured water into one of the tin cups on the table and took a drink. It would do no good to let anger get the best of her. She was stuck here with Mrs. Haskill.

And how was she going to pass the time? If she talked to Mrs. Haskill, she wouldn't have to listen to her. Megan sat in the chair by Mrs. Haskill's bed.

"You aren't familiar with this prairie country yet," she said, "so I'm going to tell you as much as I know about it."

Mrs. Haskill didn't object—just stared at her with a scowl—so Megan began. "The prairie is covered with long grasses all during the year. In the spring they're green and filled with wildflowers. In the summer they grow even taller—tall enough in places for an Indian to hide in. And in the fall—"

"An Indian?" Mrs. Haskill looked startled.

A thought came to Megan, and though she knew it was unkind, a spark of anger lit her imagination.

"Some of them are friendly," Megan said mischievously.

"What do you mean?"

Megan tried to make her eyes wide with innocence. "I mean that some are friendly."

"You're saying that others are not?"

Megan leaned forward and whispered, "We've all heard the stories of fearful Indian uprisings. Ben said there'd be more."

"Here?" Mrs. Haskill clutched the edge of the quilt and squirmed to a half-sitting position.

"I know very little about Indians," Megan said. "You'll have to ask your husband if you want to know more about them."

"Mr. Haskill didn't say a word about Indian uprisings!"

"They move silently through the grass," Megan said.

"The Indians?"

"Yes, and the wild animals—the wolves, especially. Have you heard them howling in the night?"

"No!"

"Ah, you're lucky, then. Of course, you're snug in here. They might come snuffling to the doorway, trying to scratch their way inside, but they're not able to sneak between the door and the sill as the rattlesnakes can."

Mrs. Haskill sat upright, her hands pressed to her chest. "Rattlesnakes? In the house?"

"Not if you're careful." She remembered something Ben had told her. "If they do get in, though, and you can stay out of their way, they might come in very handy. At least they'd eat the rats."

**87**

At that moment the door flew open. Megan leapt from her chair, overturning it, and Mrs. Haskill screamed in terror.

Mr. Haskill burst in. "What is it?" he shouted, his face blanching.

Megan hurried to reassure him. "Mrs. Haskill and I were having a fine talk about the prairie country and were just a mite startled when you entered the house so suddenly."

Mrs. Haskill had leapt out of bed and was wrapping herself in the quilt. "What is this about Indians?" she demanded.

"We've had no trouble hereabouts for some time," he said.

"The Kaw Indians used to scalp people," Megan said.

Mrs. Haskill raised one hand to her head. "Tell me truthfully, are there wolves and rattlesnakes and rats in this area?"

"Yes," he said, "but—"

"There must be rats in Boston, too," Megan said. "I know there were plenty running about the alleys and back ways in New York."

Mrs. Haskill paced back and forth, hugging the quilt around her, muttering to herself, as Mr. Haskill stared at her in amazement.

Megan tugged at Mr. Haskill's sleeve. "You can see that your wife is much improved," she said. "She has good color in her face and strength to spare."

"What's made her so upset?" Mr. Haskill asked.

"It could be my fault," Megan said, hoping the guilt she was feeling in the pit of her stomach didn't show on her face. "I told her about the prairie country. She took exception to one or two small things."

Mr. Haskill squinted down at Megan. "She mentioned

rattlesnakes. Did you frighten her with the story of the one that killed your dog?"

The thought of what had happened to Lady was painful, and Megan gave a little whimper. "That I did not," she said. "I didn't speak of it, because it still hurts too much. Lady was protecting me when she was struck by the rattler."

Mrs. Haskill's eyes were so wide that her pupils were ringed in white. "A rattlesnake killed your dog?"

As Megan saw the terror on Mrs. Haskill's face, she regretted having yielded to the temptation to get back at her. Impulsively she said, "I'm raising the pups. If you'd like to have one, I'm sure Emma would be glad to give it to you."

"Well now, that's mighty nice," Mr. Haskill said. "You'd like to have a dog around, wouldn't you, Ada?"

Mrs. Haskill thought just a moment before she answered, "I suppose I could put up with a dog. At least it would afford some protection."

Megan was so angry she almost jammed her fist through the lining of the sleeve of her coat as she pulled it on. Imagine! Not wanting a pup as a friend to love, but only for protection! She was sorry she'd offered the pup to Mrs. Haskill. She was sorry she'd come to help.

"I think your wife is well able to care for herself now," she told Mr. Haskill, "so you don't need me. I'm going home."

She ran all the way, scolding herself under her breath.

# 9

As MEGAN OPENED the door, Emma looked up from behind the worktable, her hands covered with flour. "Back so soon?" she asked. "How is poor Mrs. Haskill?"

"Up and about," Megan said. She avoided Emma's eyes, taking great pains in hanging up her coat.

"She's up already?"

"She ate two bowls of your soup. It must have been a great help."

Emma sounded puzzled. "But Farley said she had a fever."

"I don't think Mrs. Haskill was very sick," Megan told her. "I think she was just moping." She picked up Moby, who was trying to scramble over the backs of the other pups, and buried her face in his warm fur.

"Come over here, Megan," Emma said, and as Megan put the pup back into the box and obeyed, she added, "You were so kind to offer your help—especially after Mrs. Haskill—well, in any case, I'm making you a treat. Little biscuits baked with a crust of butter and brown sugar. You'll love them." She giggled. "We'll *both* love them."

"Ohhh." Megan moaned and clutched her stomach as the guilt settled there once again in a tight lump. Starting at the very beginning, she told Emma everything.

When Megan had finished, Emma thought a moment, her forehead wrinkled in concentration. "Well," she murmured, and "Hmmm," and then "Well, well," again. Finally she looked at Megan with serious eyes and said, "What you did to deliberately frighten her was wrong."

"I know," Megan said.

Emma sighed. "I remember how difficult it was to live in a dugout. It was only because I loved Ben so much, and because we had the same goals, that I could do it." Her eyes were sad as she looked at Megan. "Ada Haskill has neither love nor goals to help her adjust."

Megan could feel tears on her cheeks, and she quickly tried to wipe them away with her fingertips.

"Remember the Aesop fable about the farmer and the sticks?" Emma asked. "The farmer showed his sons how he could easily break one stick alone, but when he tied them together in a bundle, it was impossible to break them.

"Life on the prairie has many joys, but it also has terrible hardships. Who can help a woman get through the bad times if not another woman? We should never work against each other. We can only be strong by standing together."

"I'll never try to frighten Mrs. Haskill again!" Megan promised.

"Of course you won't," Emma said. "Now, help me think. How can we make amends to Ada?"

Megan wiped her eyes on her sleeve and glanced toward the brick oven set into the fireplace. The sugary fragrance of the biscuits tickled her nose. The answer was obvious. "We could give my share of the biscuits to Mrs. Haskill," she said stoically.

Emma began to wipe up the flour from the table. "If we did that, then tonight at supper Ben would ask why you weren't eating any of the biscuits, and I think that you and I are the only ones who need to know your story." She wrung out the cloth with a flourish and said, "We'll take *all* the biscuits to Ada Haskill, except for two—one for you and one for me, because we should taste them to make sure they have baked long enough."

Megan looked up quickly, in time to catch just a flash of mischief in Emma's eyes.

When the biscuits were baked, their sugar topping a deep golden crackled crust, Emma solemnly counted out two before wrapping the others in a cloth to keep them warm and tucking them into a basket.

Megan reached for the basket, but Emma put a hand in her way. "A walk will do me good. This time *I'll* pay the visit," she said. "But not before you and I have tasted the biscuits and had a cup of cold milk to go with them."

Emma chattered happily as they ate, and Megan thought how beautiful Emma was with her rosy cheeks and sparkling eyes, and how lucky she, Megan, was that Emma and Ben had chosen her.

Megan had fed Rosie, the chickens, and the hungry pups, and had tucked three potatoes into the hot fireplace ashes to bake by the time Emma returned.

She dropped her empty basket onto the floor and flung herself into the nearest chair. Her cheeks were flushed, and she breathed heavily. Megan ran to Emma and crouched before her, clasping her hands. "Are you ill?" she cried. "Please don't be ill!"

"Ill? Me? Oh, no, Megan. I'm just a bit upset. That woman—" Emma stopped and shook her head as though trying to clear it. "At least," Emma continued, as the mischief began to come back into her eyes, "I listened to all that Ada Haskill had on her mind—which was a great deal, to be sure—and I made no mention of scalpings or wolves, which took every ounce of my self-restraint!" She rocked with laughter, and Megan sat back on the floor, laughing too.

At that moment Ben poked his head in the door and studied them with a pleased expression. "I'm glad to see you two having such a good time."

Megan jumped to her feet with a shout of delight, then pulled Emma up from the chair. Emma ran to throw her arms around Ben. "You're home safely!" she cried. "I missed you!"

"The wagon's in good shape now, thanks to the black-smith," Ben said. "We won't have to worry about it this winter."

"You're hungry, aren't you?" Emma asked as she fussed over him, helping him off with his coat and gloves. "I know it's been hours since you ate all the food I packed. What did you see or hear in town? What news have you got for us?"

"Most of the talk was about the election, wondering how the states voted."

"Do they think Lincoln was elected? Did they say?" Megan asked.

"Oh, if only Kansas had statehood!" Emma said. "What was the talk about statehood? Will we get it soon?"

Ben laughed and held up both hands, palms out, in the same gesture of peace he'd made to the Indians. "I just came inside to tell you I was home. I'll feed and stable

Jay and Jimbo and be back soon. Then I'll be glad to answer all your questions."

By the time he returned, supper was on the table. Ben handed Megan a package wrapped in paper and string and said, "Before we eat, I'd like to give this to Megan. I bought it from a man who was selling most of his family's possessions before they went back east."

Megan eagerly tore off the paper and held up a carved wooden frame trimmed with gilt paint and holding a sheet of real glass. "Oh!" she cried. "It's beautiful!"

"Dear Ben, how wonderful you are," Emma murmured.

"The picture Mr. Cartwright drew of you deserves a real frame, not a homemade one," Ben told Megan. "Run and get the picture. We'll see how it looks."

Megan removed the rolled sketch from the chest where she had hidden it and brought it to Ben. He fixed it in place inside the frame and held it up for Emma and Megan to see.

"Perfect!" Emma clapped her hands together. "I love it!"

Megan studied the drawing with even more excitement than she'd felt the first time. It looked elegant inside the frame. *That girl with the solemn eyes and long dark hair is me!* she thought and felt her cheeks grow warm. "Thank you," she whispered shyly as she smiled up at Ben.

"Well, well," Ben mumbled. "I'm hungry, and the food's getting cold. Let's say grace so we can eat."

Megan didn't think about what she was eating, because what Ben had to tell them was so interesting. He was eager to report to Emma and Megan all that he had heard from the men who voiced their fears that if Abraham Lincoln were not elected, the United States would be in grave danger. "We cannot abide slavery in this

**94**

country," Ben stated, and Megan and Emma nodded in agreement.

"I hope Abraham Lincoln was elected," Megan said. "Da said he'd make things right for the country."

Ben sighed. "If he is elected, I'm afraid of what the South might do."

"If Lincoln is elected, the Southerners will just have to accept it," Emma said.

"Not necessarily," Ben said. "His name wasn't even allowed on the ballot in some states in the South. We could say there were really two elections—one in the North, and one in the South. There are strong rumors that if the electoral vote is for Lincoln, the Southern states will band together and secede from the Union."

"And form their own country?" Emma's forehead wrinkled. "The next step would truly be a civil war."

Megan leaned forward, gripping the edge of the table. "When will we know who was elected—Mr. Lincoln or Mr. Douglas?"

"Don't leave out Breckinridge, who is also with the Democratic party and very strong in the South. And there's Bell, who represents the Constitutional Union party, but I don't think that he stands a chance." Ben smiled at Megan's impatience. "Each state's electoral votes will tell the tale. Word will come fairly quickly to the cities that have telegraph, but west of the Missouri River it's going to take longer. Here in Kansas we should know in perhaps two to three weeks."

"It's hard to wait so long to find out," Emma said.

Ben leaned back in his chair. "That's not all the news I have that will interest you. There are new neighbors about six miles or so to the south of us."

Emma perked up, eyes sparkling. "Have you met them? What are they like? Tell me."

**95**

"They're Russian, near as I can figure," Ben said. "We had some trouble trying to understand each other's language. They bought the Neuman place and have it pretty well fixed up, considering the Neumans left it over a year ago."

"It's good land," Emma said, "handy to the river. Maybe they can make a go of it. I never thought the Neumans' hearts were in it."

"Well, these people—Oblinsky is their name, Maj and Nicolai Oblinsky—look as though they're ready to tackle anything, but they'll need a little help."

"What kind of help? What can we do for them?" Emma asked.

"Their sod house needs a new roof," Ben said. "I promised, if you felt it was all right for me to leave you tomorrow, to stay two days with them and help get the job done."

"Of course I want you to go," Emma said. She patted her large abdomen. "I wish I were less awkward and could go with you. But I'll send some household things."

Ben began rubbing his chin again. A worried wrinkle appeared between his eyebrows, and Megan wondered why.

"We'll be fine here," she said reassuringly. "I'll take good care of Emma."

"I'm sure you will," Ben said. "I'll ride horseback so that you'll have the other horse if you need to come for me."

Emma patted his arm. "There's no reason why we'd have to send for you. If for any reason we need help in a hurry—which we won't—we can reach Farley much faster. What's worrying you?"

"I don't know," Ben said. "It's just an odd prickle, as

your mother used to say. Maybe I don't like the idea of leaving you, Emma. Or maybe it's the weather."

As Emma and Megan looked at him with surprise, he explained, "We're well into November and long overdue for snow."

Emma got up and began to clear the plates from the table. "We've been so long overdue for rain or snow, I can't imagine you worrying about a thing like that. The sky has been clear—*too* clear, if anything. A good soaking rain would be welcome."

"Do you remember the blizzards in early 1856?" Ben asked. "They came without warning." He shrugged and looked a little sheepish. "Maybe I've been a part of this land for so long I'm beginning to feel as the land feels."

Emma stopped to pat his shoulder and rest her cheek against the top of his head. "Oh, Ben," she said, "Megan and I will be fine. Don't borrow bad luck."

*Bad luck will come to you and yours.*

Ben looked up at his wife and smiled, but Megan—the whisper of the gypsy's voice suddenly in her ears—shivered with fear.

# 10

MEGAN HUDDLED CLOSE to Emma and waved as Ben rode off on Jimbo. Although she was wearing her heavy coat and gloves, and her cap was pulled down over her ears, the morning wind stung her face with mean little nips, and she put her hands up to cover her cheeks.

"Into the house! Quickly! We're freezing out here!" Emma called. She grabbed Megan's hand, and they ran together into the house, shutting the door tightly and pulling the latchstring inside. "Poor Ben," Emma said. "The wind's growing colder." She pulled off her coat and stood in front of the fireplace, rubbing her hands together. "It would have been easier on everyone if the Oblinskys had come a few months ago, when it was warm."

Megan heard a soft thump and turned to see Patches wobbling toward her. She rushed to scoop him up and nuzzled the back of his head. "Patches managed to climb out of the box!" she said.

Emma smiled. "The puppies are growing fast."

The other pups yipped and jumped against the side of

their box, trying to join Patches, and Megan said, "I wish I hadn't promised one of them to Mrs. Haskill."

"I think a dog is just what the woman needs," Emma said. "Moby might be a good choice for her. Or Dick. Yes. Dick's such a friendly pup. Just think of all the love he'll give her. She'll soon find herself returning it."

"I hope so." Megan put Patches back into the box and cautioned him to stay there.

"We've got a great deal to do this morning," Emma said. "We'd better get busy."

Emma separated the morning's cream from the milk and added it to cream she'd kept chilled over the past two days. She poured the liquid into the barrel churn. "If you'll bring this to butter, Megan, I can start apple snitzing."

"What's snitzing?" Megan asked. "It sounds like a sneeze."

Emma laughed. "It's a short word for all the work that has to be done to apples before they can be boiled down into apple butter." Ben had brought a sack of apples up from the root cellar before he left, and now Emma dumped them out on the worktable. "They're getting mealy," she said, "no longer good enough to eat in hand." She immediately set to peeling, coring, and cutting the apples into sections. The slices went into a pot with water and spices, and Megan helped Emma carry the pot to the fireplace and hang it on one of the metal arms.

As the apple mixture began to boil and bubble, Emma watched it carefully, stirring it with a long wooden paddle.

Megan moved the dasher in the churn up and down, listening to the cream froth and splash. Soon she felt the lumps of butter begin to form and grow larger, hitting firmly against the dasher. She lifted the lid of the dasher and peered inside the churn, enjoying the tangy fragrance of the warm buttermilk.

"I think the butter's ready," she said.

"I can leave this for half a minute to take a look," Emma said. She gave her paddle a final stir through the thickening apple mixture and turned toward Megan.

At that moment Patches tumbled out of the box and sprawled in front of Emma.

"Look out!" Megan shouted.

Emma looked down, saw the pup, and tried to avoid him, but she lost her balance and fell heavily to the floor.

Megan jumped up and ran to Emma, her heart bumping loudly. "Are you hurt?" she cried.

Emma sat up and rubbed her left ankle. Megan scooped up Patches with one hand and tucked him into the box. "Stay there!" she scolded. "Look what you've done!"

"It's not his fault," Emma said. "He's a growing pup and wants to go exploring. I should have remembered that he could get out of the box and watched where I was going." She winced as she rubbed her ankle again. "I think I've sprained it. And oh—the apples!"

With a wad of toweling to protect her hands, Megan grabbed the heavy iron cooking arm and swung it out and away from the heat. "I'll get to the apples later," she said. Taking a firm grip under Emma's arms, Megan hoisted her up and into a comfortable chair.

"I'll be right back," she said and pulled on her coat.

"Where are you going?" Emma asked.

"I think I saw ice under the rim of the well," Megan told her. "I'll make a pack for your ankle to keep the swelling down." She snatched up a pan and a blunt-ended knife and ran outside.

The wind was stronger, and she struggled against it as she chipped at the ice. *More bad luck*, Megan thought angrily. *Emma is hurt because of the gypsy's curse. She made me the bad-luck penny. Look at all the trouble I cause to everyone around me! Something terrible is bound to happen to Ben and Emma if I stay here with them. But if I were to leave, I would only take harm wherever I went.*

Megan was startled to feel the sting of a hot tear on her windburned cheek. Quickly wiping it away, she scolded herself. *Shame on you, Megan Kelly. There's no time for silliness now. Emma needs you. And*—she couldn't help the little shiver that shook her spine—*you can't stop whatever trouble the curse will cause, no matter how awful it might be.*

To distract herself, Megan chipped furiously at the ice until she had half-filled the pan. She ran back to the house, and in a short time had wrapped the ice in a cloth and bound the cloth around Emma's ankle. "That's just what it needs," Emma said. "Thank you, Megan."

After a few minutes Emma tried to stand but let out a little cry and sat down again quickly. Her face was white, and tiny beads of perspiration dotted her forehead.

"Don't try to walk," Megan said.

"But I need to tend the apple butter."

"I can do that. I'm going to make you some herb tea with sugar, and then I'll cook and stir the apples until they're done. You can sit there and tell me what to do."

Emma didn't argue, so Megan knew how much pain she must be feeling. She added another log to the fire and prepared the tea. Then she swung the arm holding the apple mixture back over the fire and began to stir it slowly with the wooden paddle, just as she'd seen Emma do.

When the apples were finally cooked to a deep brown thickness, Megan brought Emma a sample. With the tip of one finger, Emma warily skimmed the glob Megan held out on the paddle. She tasted it and smiled. "That's it," she said. "Take it off the fire, and stir it now and then as long as the pan is hot, just to keep it from sticking."

Megan scooped a finger along the top of the apple butter, too, waved it quickly, and popped it into her mouth. "It's good!" she said with such surprise that Emma laughed.

"Of course it's good. Couldn't you tell by the way it smells?"

Megan shrugged and stirred the paddle once around the pot. "It's brown and strange-looking. I didn't know what to expect."

"You'll like it on your bread," Emma said. "We'll have it all winter." She stirred uncomfortably, trying to lift herself to her feet. "There is so much to do."

In an instant Megan knelt beside her and examined the ankle. It looked much less red and puffy than it had a short time earlier. "I'll bind it up for you," she said. "That will help. But you can't walk on it yet. Just let me do whatever is needed."

"There's too much," Emma told her. "There's water and firewood to bring in, and the dinner to make."

Megan removed the dripping, ice-filled pad and dried Emma's ankle. Then she took a clean strip of cloth and wound it high around the ankle and under the arch of Emma's foot, splitting the loose end in order to tie it firmly into place. She placed a pillow on the footstool and propped Emma's foot on top.

Emma sighed gratefully. "That's much better," she said. "It doesn't hurt nearly as much as it did."

Megan stood and smoothed down her skirt. "I'll start the dinner as soon as I take care of the water and wood," she said. "I may not be the best cook in the

**102**

world, but I've watched you, and I've learned your ways of doing things."

"Have you ever cooked an entire meal?"

"When I lived in New York," Megan said, "I cooked every day for my family. Ma and Frances had to work, and it was up to me to buy the food at the greengrocer's and cook the dinner and care for the two little ones." She heard the break in her voice, and she wondered how long it would be before she could think of her brothers and sisters—and especially of Ma—without such a dreadful aching hunger to see them again.

Emma took Megan's right hand and for just a moment held Megan's palm against her cheek. "How lucky we are to have you," she murmured.

Megan shuddered. If only Emma knew! "Please don't speak of luck," she whispered, and although Emma looked startled, Megan hurried into her coat and out the door to get the wood without a word of explanation.

She made sure there was plenty of wood piled in the rack that was handy to the back door, as well as a full supply in the house. Then she brought in fresh water from the well and began to cook. Emma rallied enough to complain about her lack of activity, and by late in the afternoon was hobbling about the house, with Megan trying unsuccessfully to coax her into sitting still.

The day went quickly, with many chores to do both inside and outside, and when the daylight faded, Megan was glad to relax by the fire as Emma read poems from Walt Whitman's *Leaves of Grass*. Megan didn't understand all that Mr. Whitman wrote, but she loved the sounds of his words as they marched and exploded and sometimes slipped together softly, giving shape to his ideas. She was already drowsing by the time Emma closed the book and said, "Time for bed."

**103**

"How is your ankle?" Megan murmured as she got to her feet.

"Much better," Emma said, but she limped toward her bedroom.

"I wish Ben were here," Megan said. In the distance she heard the howl of a wolf, with another joining in. The eerie wailing sound made her shiver.

Emma gave Megan a good-night hug. "I miss him, too," she said.

But that was not exactly what Megan had meant.

Concerned about Emma, Megan lay wide awake in bed, staring out her window at the clear, dark sky, so cold that the light from the stars seemed to glitter and snap. Maybe Ma could look from her window to see the same stars, she thought. Maybe Ma was thinking of Megan at the very same time that Megan was thinking of her.

The stars became blurry as their edges shimmered and dissolved. Megan turned on her side, pulling the quilt up over her ears and squeezing her eyes tightly shut against the tears. Pale, faraway speckles in a hazy sky, city stars were not the same as the large, bright ones that shone over the prairie. Ma wouldn't be looking at the stars and thinking of Megan. Ma seemed just as far away as those stars, in a strange room in a strange house that Megan couldn't even picture.

"Good-night, Ma," Megan whispered as she tugged the quilt more tightly around her. "Oh, please, please don't forget me. I'll never forget you."

Early the next morning, soon after Goliath's insistent crow, Megan hurried to the barn to feed the animals and milk the cow. The wind pushed her to a trot, and gray clouds, as thick and heavy as the stuffing in an old pillow, piled high, smothering the sky. A few flakes of snow prickled her cheeks.

Emma, in the doorway, called to Megan, her voice tight with worry. "Hurry, Megan. I'm afraid Ben was right. It looks as though we're going to have a snowstorm."

Megan tugged at the small door in the barn and managed to open it, nearly sprawling over the high sill as the wind yanked the door from her hands and slammed it shut behind her. Rosie rolled her huge eyes and shifted nervously in her stall, while Jay stamped and snorted loud breaths that hung in the cold air like miniature clouds. Megan had let the chickens into the barn the night before, and they huddled together, roosting in the hayloft, sleepy, cold, and complaining to each other in mumbled clucks and squawks.

As Megan worked—feeding the animals, cleaning their stalls, and milking Rosie—she thought about the snowstorms in New York City. Some had been miserable, with wind whipping the snow in heavy gusts down streets and around corners, even shaking the wooden building in which the Kellys lived as though trying to tear it apart. But Megan remembered Ben telling her that snowstorms in the city were nothing compared to prairie blizzards, in which the wind and snow raced and roared across the plains for days, piling up drifts higher than a man is tall, with nothing to stop their speed or break their path.

"What about you?" she asked Rosie and Jay, who turned to stare at her. "How will I take care of you?"

Jay snorted and tossed his head, and Megan thought, *How will I get to them? If the snow is as blinding as Ben described, how will I even find the barn? The animals will be safe enough in here, but someone will have to feed them, and Rosie will bawl if she becomes swollen with milk.*

Slowly Megan looked around the barn, turning until her glance fell on a long coil of rope hanging on a peg. It appeared to be about the right length, with some to spare.

The coil was heavy, but Megan managed to pull it from the peg and drag it after her as she shut the smaller barn door and let down the bar that locked it into place. She tied one end of the rope to the bar, testing it to make sure it was secure, then pulled the rest after her, playing it out as she walked. When she reached the house, she pulled the rope taut and tied the other end to the post near the back door. It made a convenient and strong guideline between the house and the barn, and she examined it with satisfaction.

The snow had begun to fall in earnest now, swirling and whipping in the driving wind. Megan was glad that she'd laid by plenty of firewood, and she hoped there was nothing she'd forgotten.

The back door opened, and Emma called, "Come inside, Megan. The storm's building. It'll be a blizzard for sure."

Megan stumbled into the house, throwing her weight against the door to close it.

"Oh, how I wish Ben were here!" Emma murmured.

For a moment Megan was frightened. "He won't set out in this just to get home to you, will he?"

Emma shook her head. "No. Ben would never do that. He's well aware of what these blizzards can be like. He'll stay with the Oblinskys until it's safe to travel."

Fear cut deep lines across Emma's forehead. Megan took her hand and said, "The house will hold up, won't it?"

"No worry about that," Emma said. "It's good and sturdy."

"The animals will be all right, too. I made sure of a way to get to the barn." Megan told Emma about the rope she had rigged, but Emma looked even more concerned.

"I don't want you going outside in this terrible weather."

Megan glanced at Emma's ankle, still a little swollen. "It's a sure thing that you're not the one to go."

"Let's hope the storm won't last long," Emma said. "We may have nothing to worry about."

But the day had become as dark as night, and Emma and Megan hurried to light the oil lamps. The wind blustered at the door, thudding against it as though someone were beating to get inside. It screamed around the corners of the house and hammered at the roof. Emma sat quietly near the fireplace, stitching pieces into the baby's quilt, but Megan could see her fingers tremble.

Megan picked up a needle and thread and a shirt of Ben's with a tear in the sleeve. She worked carefully, trying to make tiny stitches around the edge of the patch, as Ma had taught her, but she jumped in terror, often pricking her finger, each time the wind slammed against the side of the house.

The storm was worse than anything she could have imagined. She pictured it as a huge, white animal trying to claw its way into the house in order to devour them.

# 11

ON THE FIRST day Megan was able to make two trips to the barn, wading with difficulty through the snow and clinging tightly to the rope as the wind's icy claws raked her face and tried to snatch her away.

The storm had terrified the animals. Megan attempted to soothe them, but Jay was skittish, and Rosie raised her head and bawled loudly, sending some of the chickens flapping hysterically from their perch. Rosie was so frightened she'd have little milk to give. In a way, Megan thought, that would be a blessing. She could make sure that the animals had plenty of food, and she wouldn't have to worry about easing Rosie's discomfort. The animals would stay safe and snug where the storm couldn't get to them.

On the second day the snow was so deep that, even with the rope to cling to, Megan couldn't buck the strength of the wind. She stomped back into the kitchen and plopped into the nearest chair, resting her elbows on the table and her chin in her hands, frustrated at being defeated.

Emma pulled off Megan's cap and smoothed down her hair. "This is a way of life on the prairie," Emma said. "We do the best we can and recognize that there are some things we can't do, no matter how much we want to."

"But the animals—"

"They'll survive. They're stronger than you think." Emma tucked a finger under Megan's chin and lifted her head. As their eyes met, Emma smiled at her. "So are you, Megan. You've got an inner strength I hadn't suspected. You're a survivor, too."

To her surprise Megan suddenly pictured the Haskills' dugout, mounded over with snow, nothing to show that anyone lived in that burrow inside the hill but the black stovepipe poking up like a dirty smudge against the whiteness. "I wonder if Mrs. Haskill is a survivor," she blurted.

"Oh," Emma said, her face filled with concern. "The storm will probably frighten her, but they're safe enough. Farley's been in blizzards before and knows how important it is to keep the stovepipe from getting covered with snow. We won't worry about Ada and Farley, Megan. They'll get through this with no harm done."

"I'm sure they will," Megan said, but she knew she hadn't sounded any more convinced than Emma had.

Early the third morning, a sudden deep silence settled over the land. It woke Megan with as much of a start as if it had been a loud noise. The wind had stopped, and she leaned on the sill of her bedroom window, rubbing away the crystals of frost, to see the prairie glittering in the thin, early light. Megan thrilled to the sight as though it had been created for her alone.

Finally, reluctantly, she left the window. There was

work to be done. Emma was still asleep, so Megan dressed as silently as possible, pulling on her heavy coat, gloves, and boots. She could get to the barn now, care for the animals, and bring back some warm milk for Emma—if Rosie would cooperate.

In spite of the storm the rope was still securely in place. Megan clung to it thankfully, taking one slow step at a time, sinking into the snow and shivering as it fell into the tops of her boots. She had to scoop some of the snow away from in front of the high sill in order to open the small door. The big doors, flush with the ground, couldn't be opened until the drifts of snow had been shoveled away.

Megan would have liked to have left the small door ajar, just to let in light, but the cold air would have quickly chilled the barn, so she shut it tightly and lit one of the lanterns.

She talked soothingly to Rosie and Jay, but they shifted nervously and rolled their eyes. Jay laid back his ears and whinnied.

"What is it, Jay?" Megan asked. She could feel him tremble as she stroked his neck. "The storm's over. There's nothing to be afraid of now."

She cleaned his stall hurriedly, eager to fork in fresh hay and care for Rosie. At first Rosie stood passively as Megan milked her, but she suddenly raised her head, as though aware of a sound only she could hear, and swung her rump sideways, almost knocking over both Megan and the pail of milk.

Megan grabbed the pail and scrambled out of the way. "What's the matter with you?" she demanded. Trying to figure out what was spooking the animals, Megan listened carefully. But Jay let out another high-pitched whinny, and with both animals stomping and snorting and the chickens setting up a racket of squawks and flapping wings, Megan couldn't hear a thing.

"I think I know what your problem is. You're restless," she said. "Well, I'm not sure what Ben would do with you, but I *am* sure that the snow's too deep for you to be put out to pasture. It's my way of thinking you'll be better off staying here in the barn."

Satisfied that she could do no more for them, Megan put out the lantern, picked up the bucket, and pushed the small door open.

The sun had come out, and its glare on the snow blinded her for a moment. She stood still in the doorway, letting her eyes adjust to the brightness. She could see her deep tracks in the snow, but they were now criss-crossed by other sets of tracks. Puzzled, she stared at the trampled area. The animal—or animals, because there were rows of tracks that looked as though they wound around and around the barn—had made these marks while she was inside. The prints were the size of large dog paws. Where would dogs have come from?

To her right she heard a snuffling sound. There, standing just a few feet away, were two large gray prairie wolves. Their eyes gleamed yellow as they stared at her without blinking, and their lips were parted, tongues lolling to one side. Breath rose from their nostrils in wisps of steam.

For one heart-stopping moment Megan stared back at the wolves, unable to move, unable to look away. Then one of them shifted a paw just a fraction of an inch. Its chest muscles tensed and its shoulders lowered, and Megan realized that it was getting ready to spring. With a yelp of terror, she leapt back into the barn, set down the pail so hard that the milk sloshed over the side, and slammed the door shut.

Panting and shaking, Megan tried to think. She couldn't stay in the barn. She had to get back to the house. Emma would be up by now, making breakfast, expecting her to return soon. If she didn't appear, then Emma would come out looking for her, and the wolves would be waiting. No!

She searched the contents of the barn for some sort of protection, wishing with all her heart that she had the Henry rifle with her. *Don't waste time wishing for things that can't be*, Megan scolded herself. *Think! What is there here at hand that can help you?*

Her glance fell on the pitchfork, the hoe, and the metal rake, and for a moment she was hopeful. But she shook her head. Those wolves were huge animals and most probably very hungry. She wouldn't be strong enough to beat them off with a pitchfork. They could circle in and . . . She shuddered. They wouldn't be afraid of a mere pitchfork.

What *would* they fear? On the chest against the wall stood the lantern where she had left it, and with a sigh of relief she knew what she could do.

As the wolves snuffled at the door and the animals in the barn moved about uneasily, Megan found a cloth feed sack, and wrapped it tightly around the metal end of the hoe. Over the cloth she wrapped large clumps of hay, until the hoe looked like a fat, gigantic broom. Then, carefully, she dribbled oil from the lantern onto the hay.

She leaned against the door, her heart thumping loudly. She could still hear the wolves scratching and growling on the other side. She had to get them away from the door!

Megan pounded on the door with all her might, hoping that would startle them for an instant. Then, with flint and steel, she set fire to the oil on the hay and threw the door wide, poking the flaming brand outside.

The wolves backed off a few feet, wary of the fire. "Yaaah!" Megan yelled at them. Waving the brand at them with her right hand, she reached back with her left, pulled the door shut, and dropped the beam across it. Now the animals would be safe inside the barn, but she was unprotected, with only the fiery stick between herself and the hungry wolves. She gasped in air so cold that her lungs hurt and yelled, "Emma!"

As she struggled through the snow toward the house, holding the rope with one hand, the wolves moved close enough so that she could see the reflection of the fire in their eyes. The hay disappeared in a final crackle, flinging burning speckles upon the snow, but the cloth still burned steadily, and the pole itself had ignited. The wolves stayed just out of range of the flickers of flame, but they moved more easily in the heavy snow than Megan could.

Megan felt as though she were in a nightmare. She tried to hurry, but her feet sank with each step, and if it hadn't been for her grasp on the rope, she would have fallen. When she faltered, one of the wolves darted toward her, coming low to snap and snarl, while the other menaced her from the other side. With a yell, Megan thrust the burning pole at them, swinging it wildly, and they jumped back, their red tongues hanging out and their sharp teeth gleaming.

The fire on the pole was down to a dull glow. It would soon go out. She would never reach the house. "Emma!" Megan screamed again.

"I'm here. Don't move!" she heard Emma call.

A loud crack shattered the air. The wolf nearest to

Megan leapt upward, twisted, and fell on its side, its blood a dark red blot melting into the snow.

"Come, Megan! Hurry!" Emma shouted.

Megan looked up. Emma was standing in the doorway, sighting along the Henry rifle toward the second wolf. Megan didn't stop to watch. With all her strength she hurled herself through the snow toward the house. As she staggered past Emma and over the doorsill, the gun exploded a second time, so close that the sound made her ears ring.

Emma half-fell inside and slammed the door as Megan pulled down the bar. They clung together, trembling, tears mingling and arms tightly wrapped around each other.

After a long moment they both began talking at once.

"I was afraid you'd come outside."

"I heard you cry out and saw through the window what was going on."

"I didn't know you were there with the rifle."

"I didn't want to distract you. If you'd looked up before I had a clear shot—"

"I was so frightened! What if the fire had burned out too fast?"

"Dear little Megan, you were very brave."

"Brave? I can't stop shaking!"

Emma pulled Megan's head to rest on her shoulder and soothed her, stroking her hair back from her forehead. "There may be more wolves out there, hungry enough to try desperate measures, or those two may have been lost from their pack, looking for food on their own. We don't know, so we'll stay safely inside."

Megan relaxed, loving the closeness with Emma, but suddenly a thought struck her and she pulled away. "Oh, the milk!" she cried. "I forgot it. I'll go back and get it."

**114**

As Emma broke into laughter, Megan realized what she had said and clapped her hands to her cheeks. The two of them rocked back and forth, laughing away the last of their fear.

Emma wiped her eyes and said, "Time to get busy, Megan. There's much to be done before Ben gets home, and he'll head this way as soon as the road is passable."

For the rest of the day, as they cleaned and cooked and sewed, both Megan and Emma avoided looking outside in the direction of the barn. At night, when the house was dark and she could hear wolves howling in the distance, Megan tossed until her bed was a rumpled mess, unable to fall asleep.

Ben came home early in the afternoon of the next day. Megan and Emma told him the story, their words spilling over each other.

Ben hugged them both. "What bad luck that I was away from you at a time like this!"

Bad luck? Until he said that, Megan hadn't thought of the old woman. Of couse, this was more of the gypsy's work. Megan looked away, unable to meet Ben's eyes. What trouble and sorrow would the curse next bring?

# 12

To MEGAN'S SURPRISE the snow began to melt quickly, leaving shrunken, grayed drifts where the sun couldn't reach. In the open areas, battered clumps of blackened grass and hard-packed ground mingled with patches of snow.

Ben had gone to check on the Haskills the day after he returned home. He came back to report to Emma and Megan that the Haskill home was so filled with misery he could hardly wait to leave.

"Poor Ada's had some hard surprises," Emma said. "First the house, and now the blizzard. But I think she'll come around. I'll bake some gingerbread and Megan can take it to her." She looked at the puppies, in the new box with higher sides where Ben had moved them. "In two or three weeks Dick will be ready to move to a new home. A puppy to love will do wonders for Ada."

Megan had her doubts about that and was more inclined to pity Dick than Mrs. Haskill, but she remembered what Emma had said about women on the prairie needing one another's support and kept her thoughts to herself.

When she carried the basket of hot gingerbread to the Haskills', Megan was surprised to find the room cluttered and the dishes unwashed. Clothes lay on the floor, and the bed was a tangle. For a few moments Mrs. Haskill stared through Megan as though she couldn't place her. Then she brushed back the loose, stringy wisps of hair that had escaped from the bun at the back of her neck and said to Megan, "Would you like to sit down?"

Wishing she could say, "No, thank you," and escape for home, Megan put the gingerbread on the table, shoving aside two tin plates with dried food on them to make room. She took off her coat, cap, and gloves and dutifully sat on one of the slatted chairs near the stove, opposite Mrs. Haskill.

Mrs. Haskill stared into space, pulling her shawl tightly around her shoulders, and said nothing. Megan, her nose itching uncomfortably from the smoke and the stale, sour air in the room, finally asked, "Wouldn't you like a piece of gingerbread? Emma baked it, and it's very good."

As though she hadn't heard Megan, Mrs. Haskill mumbled, "No one should have to live like this."

"Mr. and Mrs. Browder did," Megan said. "They lived in a dugout until their farm began to prosper. Then they were able to build their house. Now they use their old dugout as a root cellar and a place to hide when the spring tornadoes come."

Mrs. Haskill lifted her head and stared at Megan. "Tornadoes?"

Oh, no! She'd done it again, and this time she hadn't meant to.

Megan hopped to her feet. "Let me bring you some gingerbread. It's still warm. Emma sent it right from the oven." She looked into the cupboard but couldn't find a single clean dish, so she took a gingerbread square from the basket and placed it on the palm of Mrs. Haskill's left hand.

"I hadn't bargained on this." Mrs. Haskill's voice was a dull whisper.

"I couldn't find a plate," Megan began to explain.

But Mrs. Haskill interrupted. "It's not fair. I'm used to a better life," and Megan realized that the woman hadn't even noticed the gingerbread she was holding.

There was no point in trying to make conversation with Mrs. Haskill, so Megan set to work. There was a full basket of wood and dried cow chips next to the stove, so she opened the iron lid and added enough fuel to stir up a good-size fire. Apparently Mr. Haskill had brought in fresh water, because the crock was full. She ladled some into the kettle and set it on the stove. While she waited for the water to come to a boil, she made the bed and picked up the clothes from the floor. They needed to be washed, but that was an all-day job she wasn't ready to tackle. Megan swept and tidied, and when the water was hot enough she poured some into a large pan, added a little cold water, and began to wash the dishes.

She washed and dried a tin cup first, hunted through the cupboard until she found some of Emma's herbal tea, and prepared a steaming cup for Mrs. Haskill. "Here," she said, placing the cup on the table next to Mrs. Haskill's chair. "Eat your gingerbread and drink your tea. You'll feel much better."

As Mrs. Haskill mechanically obeyed, Megan went back to washing the dishes. Before long they'd been put away, and the table had been scrubbed. At last the room looked the way it was supposed to. Mrs. Haskill had drunk the tea and eaten every crumb of her piece of gingerbread, and now even she looked better. There was more color in her cheeks, and she actually turned to Megan as though she saw her.

"Please tell Mrs. Browder that her gingerbread was quite satisfactory," Mrs. Haskill said.

"Quite satisfactory!" Megan almost choked on the words.

"Yes. Considering the rustic conditions and poor choice of ingredients she has to work with, Mrs. Browder has managed to make her gingerbread fairly tasty." She nodded. "Please convey my gratitude."

"Yes, ma'am," Megan mumbled. She waited for Mrs. Haskill to notice the changed condition of her house, but Mrs. Haskill merely said, "I mustn't keep you from your chores. I'm sorry you didn't have time to stay for tea."

Megan hurried into her coat, buttoning it askew but unwilling to stop and rebutton it. Jamming on her cap and gloves, she escaped from the Haskill house and ran almost all the way home.

Back in the Browders' kitchen, Megan flung herself into the nearest chair, gulping for breath.

Emma hurried to her side. "Is something wrong, Megan?"

"I ran," Megan managed to gasp.

One of Emma's eyebrows rose as she stared at Megan questioningly. "Are you all right?"

Megan nodded, breathing more easily now. "It's cold and clear and a nice day for running." She took off her coat, stuffing the cap and gloves into the pockets, and hung it on the coat rack.

"Tell me about the Haskills," Emma said.

"Mr. Haskill wasn't at the house," Megan said, "so I didn't see him. Mrs. Haskill ate a piece of your gingerbread and said it was—umm—I don't remember the exact words. 'Very tasty.' I think that was it. She said to thank you."

---

**119**

"I'm glad she liked the gingerbread." Emma looked pleased. "Was she cordial to you this time? How did your visit go? Tell me."

Megan could see no reason not to tell Emma most of the story, so she described the dirty house and how she had cleaned it. "Mrs. Haskill doesn't care about her house," Megan said.

"That's a bad sign." Emma sighed. "Poor Ada. We must try to make things easier for her. I wish I knew how."

"I don't think there's a way in the world to make things better for Mrs. Haskill," Megan said. "No matter what I do for her, it doesn't please her. I don't like helping her, not one little bit." There. Now that the words had been spoken, Megan sighed with relief.

"I'm sure, knowing you, Megan, that you helped Ada the same way you would have if you *had* liked her. Didn't you?"

"Well, yes. That I did," Megan answered.

"Then it comes to the same thing."

"But not the way I feel about it. That's not the same."

"Is the way you feel as important as what you do?"

"Yes! No." Megan flopped into a nearby chair. "I don't know. I'll have to think about it," she said, even though she had to admit to herself that Emma was probably right.

Later, Emma repeated Megan's account of Ada Haskill's problems to Ben.

"It's obvious that Ada's lonely," he said. "We'll invite them when the Parsons come to visit, and we can certainly share our Christmas with them. That might help."

"Of course," Emma promptly answered, but there was little enthusiasm in her voice.

What Ben had said was right and the only neighborly

thing to do, Megan knew, but Christmas was going to be hard enough to bear, so far away from her family. Having Ada Haskill around would truly turn the holiday into a miserable day for everyone. With all her heart Megan wished that Mrs. Haskill would just go away.

Her wish had been so strong that Megan felt both shock and guilt when two days later the Haskills drove up in a wagon heaped high with their household possessions. Emma's down pillow rested on the seat between them. Behind the wagon a cow was tied.

"We're leaving Kansas," Mr. Haskill said. "It's too hard a life here for a lady like Ada."

Mrs. Haskill, her beautiful hat pinned firmly in place, glanced at her husband with approval.

"Granted, it takes a lot of hard work," Ben said in a mild tone.

Mr. Haskill hunched his shoulders defensively. "There've been plenty who've had the good sense to leave," he said.

"That's right," Emma echoed, and Mrs. Haskill glanced at her with grateful surprise. "It's important for the two of you to put your marriage first. Where are you going? What will you do?"

"We may try Ohio," Mr. Haskill said. "Maybe we'll settle even farther east."

"In a city," Mrs. Haskill added firmly. "Mr. Haskill is skilled at many things. He should have no trouble finding well-paid work to do." Mr. Haskill's cheeks grew red with embarrassment.

Ben quickly tried to change the subject. "What about your land, Farley? Are you going to just abandon it?"

Mr. Haskill pulled off a glove, reached into an inner pocket of his outer coat, and tugged out a folded piece of paper. "If you want to take it over to add to your own, I'm giving you the right. It's all written down here. Should be legal enough."

"But you might be able to sell it."

"Who'd want it?" Mr. Haskill jerked his chin toward the back of the wagon. "The cow's yours, too, and the chickens—only I left them on the place. I figured you'd have an easier time collecting them and getting them over here than I would."

"That's a mighty fine gift, Farley," Ben said.

Mrs. Haskill sat up straighter. "We couldn't put a price on them, but it would help if you could pay a little something toward—"

Mr. Haskill's eyes blazed, surprising all of them, as he snapped, "I said they were a *gift*, Ada!"

"The Browders are better off than we are," Mrs. Haskill grumbled at her husband. "Look at them—a real house, and they've even got an Irish to help with chores."

There was a long moment of echoing silence.

"I'm sorry," Mr. Haskill said, and his shoulders drooped. "I've been proud to have you as neighbors, Ben and Emma, and you, too, Megan. You've all been good to us. Thanks for all you've done and given us." He broke off and reached down to hand Emma her pillow. "You're a good, kind woman."

Ben quickly untied the cow, and Mr. Haskill turned the wagon, heading toward the road. He twisted around once, to wave good-bye, but Ada Haskill sat stiffly and never looked back.

As Ben led the cow to the barn, Emma put one arm around Megan's shoulders and the other around her pillow and hugged them both tightly. "Please don't feel unhappy about what that terrible woman said."

"I don't give any importance to what she said," Megan

---

**122**

answered, "but now you have no near neighbor, and that's my fault. I made a selfish wish that Mrs. Haskill would go away, and the wish came true."

"That's not your doing. It's poor Farley's misfortune that he married a woman who has no faith in him or in what he can make of himself."

"There's more to it than that." Megan shivered.

Emma looked at her with concern and said, "Let's not stand out here in the cold."

As soon as the door had shut behind them, Megan said, "There's something I must tell you. Bad things happen because I'm under a gypsy's curse. I'm a bad-luck penny for sure." Tearfully, angrily, she told Emma about the old gypsy woman and how her ominous words had haunted Megan's life.

"So that's what the gypsy in your dream was all about," Emma said.

"Look at all the misfortunes I've brought on this family!" Megan said, and took a deep, shuddering breath. "I think you should send me away."

Emma reached out to hold Megan tightly. "Nonsense! We could never send you away."

"But if I bring bad luck—"

"Life is not easy. We all have problems—even tragedies—to deal with, and luck has nothing to do with it. 'Bad luck' is only a superstitious excuse for those who don't have the wit to deal with the problems of life. And you've proved that you have the wit and intelligence and cleverness to handle any crisis."

Megan raised her head, and Emma smiled. "Don't keep stumbling over what some addled old woman said. Believe in yourself. *I* believe in you."

"I—I'm not sure that I can."

"Of course you can." Emma paused, then asked, "What did your mother say about the gypsy's curse?"

"Ma said it was only foolishness."

"She was right, but it's even worse than just foolishness. Think about what I said, Megan. You're a practical young lady. Isn't trusting in your own good mind better than hiding behind a gypsy woman's silly superstition?"

Megan was disturbed. "Hiding? From what?"

"Maybe from something inside yourself. Only you can discover the answer to that."

Megan shook her head, thoroughly confused. "I don't exactly understand what you mean, but I'll think about it," she promised.

Daylight hours grew much shorter, pale sunlight giving way to deep blue twilight. The long December evenings were spent by candlelight and lantern light. Megan took turns with Emma in reading aloud, and she proudly wrote painstaking letters to Ma and to Frances, Mike, Danny, Peg, and Petey, ready to mail whenever the opportunity arose.

Megan was aware that long after she went to bed each night, Emma sat by the fire, working with her needle. The baby quilt had been finished, but when Megan asked Emma what she was sewing, Emma just smiled.

Ben had secrets, too. Sometimes he went back to the barn after dinner, and Megan occasionally could hear the sounds of a saw and hammer.

The approach of Christmas drew Megan's thoughts repeatedly to the past. The children in her family had never had much for Christmas; often they'd been given an orange or an apple for a treat, and maybe a shiny penny. But what Megan remembered was the love they shared, and their happiness at being together. On Christmas Day—the only day in the year that none of them had to work at jobs outside their home—the Kellys would go to church. They dressed in their best, such as it was—and sat among the fine ladies and gentlemen. To Megan's way of thinking, none of the ladies, with their fur muffs and velvet skirts, was half as beautiful as Ma, with her hat balanced on top of her swirl of bright red hair, and none of the gentlemen who strolled down the church steps, brandishing their silver-topped canes and clapping their elegant top hats on their heads, could match Da's strong, dark handsomeness.

The fragrance of candle wax, the wonderful music that swirled to the high-domed ceiling, the painted statues that seemed to smile down on those at prayer—Megan would hug them to herself, wrapped in the beauty and joy that were so special to Christmas. But all that was left of these Christmases were memories, and there could never be another Christmas for all of them together.

Each night, as Megan lay in bed, a wrapped hot stone from the Browders' fireplace warming her toes, she would squeeze her eyes shut and try hard to fall asleep. She'd hear Emma humming softly as she worked and wish it were Ma. She'd sensibly remind herself that she had much to be grateful for, that Emma and Ben were good, kind people, but in her mind Megan would see her family and long for them with such agony that she'd have to press the quilt against her mouth to keep from sobbing aloud.

*I want to go home!* Megan cried to herself over and over, even though she knew she couldn't. Her family had been separated forever. Even the room she had known as home was gone. And all because she was a bad-luck penny. The gypsy had said so. She reminded herself of what Emma had told her, that her own wit and clever-

**125**

ness were stronger than any gypsy curse, and over and over she asked herself, *What could I be hiding from?* But the answer never came, and deep in her heart was a growing dread that there was even more bad luck in store.

# 13

ONE EVENING CLEM Parker came by to join the Browders at dinner and share the news that Abraham Lincoln had been elected. Although Ben rejoiced, Mr. Parker shook his head sadly. "They say the Southern states are ready to pull out of the Union." He took a second helping of apple butter, piling it high on his bread. "President Buchanan's not strong enough to hold them. Between the election and March fourth, Buchanan's a lame duck."

"A *what*?" Megan asked.

Even Emma couldn't keep from laughing. "It does sound comical," she said. "But a lame duck can neither run nor fly. He isn't much good to himself or to anyone else. And that's the way it is with a man who holds a political office that someone else is soon going to take over."

Megan shrugged. "I understand. I just think that it's silly to call a man a lame duck. It wouldn't surprise me to learn that Mr. Aesop's behind that name and the story to go with it."

Mr. Parker clapped a hand to his pocket and widened

his eyes in mock surprise. "Bless me if I didn't almost forget. Speaking of news from back East—" He pulled out a packet of envelopes. "Here's the mail from the post office in St. Joe." He handed the top two letters to Ben. Then he looked at Megan and smiled. "My, my. It seems the rest are for this young lady."

Megan leapt from her chair and tried not to snatch the letters from Mr. Parker's hand, barely remembering to say thank you as she took them. There was a letter from Ma dated one month ago, and one from Frances, and even a letter from Mike!

Emma gave Megan a smile and a pat and sent her off to read her letters. Megan lit the lamp in her room, then sat cross-legged on her bed. She laid the letters on her lap, touching each with her fingertips, tracing the familiar handwriting, making the moment last longer in order to treasure it more.

She opened Ma's letter first. Megan had practiced every day at reading the cursive writing sheets Emma had prepared for her, so although some of Ma's words were hard to make out, she worked on the sounds of the syllables until they made sense. Megan was delighted that she could read the letters without asking for help.

Ma had a funny story to tell about the cook in the great house where she worked, who accidentally mixed the salt and sugar one morning, creating a rumpus throughout the household. "At least it woke up the sluggards," Ma wrote. She went on to tell about the eldest son of the family, who every day slumped at the breakfast table, his chin almost in his porridge, grumbling about having to wake up so early to accompany his father to his uptown office. "After a big gulp of coffee flavored with lots of salt, he went to work with his eyes wide open."

Megan smiled at the stories, even though she ached

with loneliness for Ma. Again and again she read the letter, then closed her eyes, trying to picture the people Ma wrote about, trying to picture Ma herself at the table in the big kitchen writing her letter.

Megan opened Frances Mary's letter next. Petey had grown at least two inches, Frances insisted, and had been allowed to ride the gentlest of the horses. "I can drive the team by myself," Frances wrote. This was exciting news, and Megan wanted to know more about it, so she was disappointed that the rest of the letter went on and on about someone named Johnny Mueller. Megan read that part of the letter twice and didn't understand why Frances had filled most of the sheet of paper writing about this boy. Was he really that special? Nothing Frances had written led Megan to believe so. She shrugged. Lots of boys could whistle through their teeth.

As Megan read Mike's letter about the Friedrich family she gasped in indignation, then grunted with anger. Finally she let out such a joyful whoop that Emma popped into the doorway, her eyes wide.

"What's the matter?" Emma asked.

Megan waved Mike's letter and laughed. "Oh, there's so much I have to tell you about Mike!" she said. "Some of it's dreadful enough to chill your bones, but there's a good part. Mike's living now with that fine Captain Taylor we met on the train! The captain and his wife took Mike to live with them at Fort Leavenworth! Imagine! Mike was always so excited about the West, and now he's living on a real army post!"

Emma grinned with Megan and held out a hand. "Don't forget the letters you've written to your family. Better give them to Clem. He's almost ready to leave."

Megan scooped the letters from the top drawer in the little chest and quickly printed Mike's new address on

**129**

the one she'd written to him. She had some exciting stories to tell her family, too. Just wait until they read about her escape from the wolves!

The snow had melted completely by the time the Parsons came for a visit. The children hopped down from the wagon bed and ran shrieking toward Megan.

"We brought candy!" Teddie shouted.

"Mama made it!" Thea screeched.

"Vinegar taffy, and I helped pull it, and Thea couldn't because Mama was afraid she'd drop it because she did last time and—"

"No fair! You told, and you promised Mama you wouldn't!"

Thea raised a small fist, but Megan skillfully intercepted it. Holding one of Thea's hands and one of Teddie's, she led them into the house. Thea squealed when Moby scampered to her, and both children dove to the floor to play with the puppies, not taking the time to remove their heavy coats and caps.

"Would you like a pup for your very own?" Emma asked them.

"Oh yes! This one!" Thea shouted as Moby's pink tongue licked her face.

The Parsons brought not only the taffy, which was so wondrously chewy that Teddie lost a loose front tooth, but also a Christmas cake thick with currants, a cured ham, and loaves of dark wheat bread. Will Parson carefully unwrapped his fiddle. "We'll have some music of an evening," he said.

Emma and Nelda Parson chattered to each other without stopping from the time Nelda entered the house. Occasionally they added their opinions to the men's conversations about prospects for their spring crops,

---

**130**

new settlers in the territory, Kansas politics, and the unrest in the South which President Buchanan couldn't, or wouldn't, handle. For the most part they talked eagerly, hungrily, to one another about their own concerns, the many things only a woman would understand. Megan recognized the loneliness that caused them to bubble over with words and shut out everything else, so she kept Teddie and Thea busy with games and stories.

That night Nelda and Will took Megan's bed, and Megan bedded down with the Parson children on pallets near the fireplace. With just a minimum of whispering and giggling, the two little ones fell asleep, but Megan lay awake, thinking over the busy day. There had been laughter and fun, and the music was the grandest treat of all, but she couldn't help thinking of her own brothers and sisters. Why was there always sorrow, like the darkest shadow of night, slipping in to turn laughter into tears? She hunched down under the quilt, rolling into a ball, picturing her family and hoping with all her might that they were happy. She wondered how they would be celebrating Christmas. Would they miss her as much as she missed them?

For some unknown reason, as she saw Peg in her mind, she shivered. Did it mean something good or something bad? Why hadn't Danny and Peg sent her a letter? Couldn't someone in their new family have written for them? Surely they were all right. Or were they? Oh, how she wished there had been a letter from Danny and Peg!

The next morning, while Ben and Will were working in the barn, Teddie screamed, "There's a man coming!" and dashed toward the road. The others hurried after him, watching the large, bulky figure on horseback approach.

The man raised a hand in greeting and shouted, "Halloo!"

"It's Marshal John Avery," Ben said, and called back a greeting.

The marshal swung from his horse in the Browders' front yard and pulled off his hat. After he had greeted the women and had been introduced to Megan, he clapped it back onto his head.

"Come inside, John," Emma said. "You could probably use a hot cup of coffee and something to eat."

He shook his head. "Thanks, but I haven't got time. I just stopped by to see if Ben would lend me a hand. I'm glad to see Will is here, too. We can pick up Farley and—"

"Farley left the territory," Ben said.

Marshal Avery shook his head slowly. "I never thought the land would be too much for Farley. The man had real purpose."

"Farley got married," Ben said, "and he and his wife decided to go back east."

Megan waited, but neither Ben nor Emma added any information about Ada.

The marshal didn't seem curious. He just said, "I got word from Joe Dawson, marshal in the territory east of here, askin' me to look out for a man name of Cully Napes. Dawson personally thinks Napes headed south toward Texas, but someone who knew Napes was sure he'd travel in this direction, and Dawson has got to check it out."

"What did this Cully Napes do?" Ben asked.

"Killed a man," Marshal Avery said, and Megan felt a cold chill in the pit of her stomach. "Napes and two other rowdies got to actin' up over near the Missouri border," the marshal continued. "They was tryin' to bully some folks in a tavern and, whether on purpose or accidental, set fire to the building. Everyone got out, but the tavern owner went after the troublemakers with a rifle. Unfortunately, Napes is a good shot drunk or sober. Before the man could do more than lift his rifle, Napes killed him."

Emma gasped. "That's terrible!"

"I hope they find him!" Nelda was indignant.

"What does he look like?" Will asked.

The marshal pursed his lips and squinted. "He's young and stocky and tall—close to six feet. Black hair, with long moustaches. No beard. Dressed like just about anybody, 'cept for a fringed leather jacket sort of like those the mountain men wear."

"What about the other two men?" Megan asked.

"They arrested the two who were with Napes, but Napes got away. My job right now is to get some volunteer help, fan out, and take a look for any signs he may be in these parts. And that's why I'm here."

"We'll go with you," Ben said. "I'll get my rifle."

As Ben and Will strode toward the house, Megan could see the worry in Emma's and Nelda's eyes. She squeezed shut her own eyes in fear, only to see the gypsy, laughing and pointing at her. Quickly she opened them again to drive off the taunting face, but she couldn't escape the thought that something awful was about to happen, and somehow it was all her fault.

Megan wanted to cling to Ben's arm and beg, "Please don't go! Nothing bad can happen to you, because Emma needs you." But she knew no one else would understand why she was so afraid, so she had no choice but to follow Emma's lead and, without a protest, watch the men ride away.

"It won't take long," were the marshal's last words to

the women. "I'll have your husbands back here before nightfall."

Megan watched the dust kicked up by the horses' hooves swirl and shiver and settle. She came to with a start, though, when Emma tucked a finger under her chin and smiled at her. "Don't look so worried, Megan. That horrible Cully Napes is probably far away from here by now. Ben and Will will be all right."

"I—I just wish they didn't have to go with the marshal."

"Where people live far from each other, with wide spaces in between, they need each other all the more. No one who refused to give help when it was asked would be able to exist on the prairie."

Nelda wrapped her shawl more tightly around her shoulders and shivered. "It's so cold! Why are we standing out here, when we could be warm in the house?"

Her children raced ahead to see who could be first inside, but Megan stepped back. "No one's gathered the eggs yet," she said, "and since I already have my coat on, I'll do it."

Emma smiled her thanks and hurried after Nelda, while Megan went to the coop. The hens, sleepy and cold, had burrowed into their nests, and there were eggs, warm against Megan's fingers as she scooped them into her basket.

She went toward the barn, intending to make sure that Ben and Mr. Parson hadn't left any unfinished chores for her to do, but she stopped suddenly as a movement just inside the small door caught her attention. She looked carefully, straining to see, but there was only quiet shadow. It wasn't unusual for the door to be left open during the day, so there was nothing suspicious in that.

Could one of the children be hiding there? No. The children were inside the house. She could hear them laughing and shrieking as their mother tried to raise her voice over theirs, shouting to them to calm down.

An animal? With a gasp she remembered the wolves, seeing in her mind their terrifying, gleaming eyes. But a wolf would have sprung out at her by this time. They'd heard no wolves for weeks. It couldn't have been a wolf.

Megan began to doubt she had seen anything at all. It had probably been a trick of the light, and her imagination had taken over. But instead of going into the barn, she went back to the house.

As she placed the basket of eggs on the table, she glanced up at the gun rack. Ben had taken his favorite rifle, but the Henry rifle was still in place. Quietly, so she wouldn't unnecessarily alarm anyone, Megan took the rifle from the rack, checked to make sure it was loaded, and placed it near the door behind the coatrack, where it was hidden by the layers of coats. She'd have to keep a special watch to make sure the children didn't discover it, but she felt safer with it hidden and close at hand.

Just then Teddie whizzed past her. He flung open the door and raced outside, Thea on his heels. They had dashed down the step and across the yard before Megan could stop them.

"You're it! You're it!" Thea screamed so loudly that neither of them could hear Megan shout, "Come back!"

"Megan." At the fireplace Emma straightened, one hand pressed to the small of her back. "Will you watch the children? They're so excited, there's no telling what—"

But Teddie and Thea were racing back, screaming, "There's a man hiding in the barn!"

# 14

MEGAN RAN TO the children, grabbed their hands, and pulled them toward the house, but their short legs were no match for the man's long strides. By the time Megan reached the door, he was beside her, roughly shoving all of them into the room.

"Shut the door!" he yelled at Megan, brandishing a large handgun.

Nelda shrieked and started toward her children. Emma raised a stirring paddle as though she could protect them with it. Her face pale with fear, she shouted at the man, "Leave those children alone!"

Teddie and Thea ran to their mother and clung to her, and she stooped to wrap her arms around them.

Megan was frozen where she stood, too frightened to move, but when the man yelled, "I told you to shut that door!" she quickly obeyed.

This had to be Cully Napes. He fit the marshal's description. But the marshal had left something out. Napes was so dirty that he smelled like a privy. Megan wrinkled her nose in disgust.

He waved his gun again as he barked, "All of you—get over to that side of the room. Now!" He grabbed Megan by the shoulder and gave her a shove that almost knocked her off her feet.

Emma's voice was firm. "We'll do as you say. There's no need for you to behave like that."

"Behave like that?" he mocked. "You sound like a schoolmarm." He pulled Ben's chair up to the fireplace and dropped into it, stretching out his legs, his gun laid across his lap. His glance swept the room, and he smiled when he saw the empty gun rack. "I saw your menfolk ride off with the marshal," he said. "Any others around this place? Any hired hands?"

"No," Emma said. Pink blotches stood out on her pale cheeks, but she spoke quietly and calmly, trying to hide her fear.

"Fix me something to eat," Napes said.

At that moment Patches scrambled to the top of the box, teetered a moment, and flopped to the floor. He picked himself up and tottered toward Napes.

"Get that dog away from me!" Napes snarled.

As though she were moving in slow motion, Megan stepped forward as Napes kicked Patches aside with the toe of his boot.

Patches let out a yelp, and both Megan and Teddie rushed toward him. Teddie scooped up Patches and tearfully yelled in Napes's face, "You're a bad man!"

Before Megan could pull Teddie away, Napes reached out and cuffed the little boy, who staggered back, shrieking in terror, and ran to his mother. Napes raised his hand again, this time aiming at Megan, but Emma rushed forward and grabbed his arm.

"Don't you dare hit the children!" she screamed at him.

Napes jumped to his feet, grabbed Emma's shoulder, and roughly shoved her across the room. Megan gasped in horror as Emma hit the wall and fell heavily to the floor.

Above the screaming of the children Megan shouted at Napes, "You dirty pig! You hurt her!"

"I told you all to stay out of my way!" Napes snapped. "Now you know I mean what I said. All of you—get down to the other end of the room!"

Nelda shepherded her children to a spot behind the kitchen table and started toward Emma.

"Stay where you are!" Napes demanded.

"She's—she's in the family way," Megan stammered, so terrified of what Napes might do next that the back of her neck was cold with sweat. "She needs help."

"What's that to me?" He pointed the gun directly at Megan. "You heard what I said. Get over there."

Megan could see into the barrel of the gun, and her knees wobbled with fright, but she took a long breath, trying to steady herself, and then another step toward Emma.

"You're asking for trouble," he growled.

Megan glanced at Emma, then back to Napes. "I know," she said, desperation giving her courage. "I *am* trouble." She turned her back on Napes and went to kneel beside Emma. Nelda came and crouched by her side.

"Don't worry, Megan," Emma murmured. "No bones broken." Emma tried to smile, but Megan could see beads of sweat pop out on Emma's forehead and knew she must be in great pain. With both of them supporting Emma, they managed to help her into a chair.

Napes tilted his chair back and grinned at them. "A lot of good that chair's gonna do you," he said to Emma.

"Hop up. Now. I want to see you two women get busy. Fix me something to eat."

The twist of his mouth so vividly reminded Megan of the gypsy's evil smile that she gasped. But she remembered what Emma had told her. "I believe in you," Emma had said. And Megan knew this was her chance to find out which was stronger—the curse of bad luck or her own good sense.

She stepped forward. "No," she said. "*I'm* the cook. I'll take care of you, Mr. Napes. Mrs. Parson can care for the others."

One of his bushy eyebrows lifted. "Oh, ho! You know my name."

"Of course," she said. She added some chips to the fire in the stove and slapped on the lid. In the large iron skillet she laid two thick slices of ham, and as the edges began to frizzle she cut some slices of cornmeal mush and fried them with the ham until they were crusty on the outside and hot on the inside. She slid the slices of mush and ham onto a plate, added a fork, and carried the plate and a small pitcher of cane syrup to Napes.

He laid the gun on his lap as he took them from her. He poured on syrup until his plate was swimming in it and handed back the empty pitcher.

"Bring me something to drink," he growled.

"What do you want?" Megan asked. "Buttermilk or water?"

"There must be somethin' better'n that around here."

"That's all we have. Take it or leave it."

He peered up at her with a scowl. "You know my name," he said. "Didn't you get the rest of it? I'm a killer."

Was he trying to frighten her—or just impress her? "That's what I heard," she answered.

"Nothin's gonna stop me from killin' again when it suits me." Napes held the plate close to his face and shoveled the ham and fried mush into his mouth as fast as he could, grunting and belching and smacking his lips. While he ate, he kept his gaze on the people in the room.

*I called him a pig. He's worse than a pig,* Megan thought. She'd seen eyes like his before. Some of the bullies in their New York neighborhood had the same mean, narrowed eyes, which darted here and there as though looking for someone else to attack. Cully Napes was a bully.

Napes turned to hand Megan the empty plate, and their eyes met. "You're not afraid of me?" he asked, and a warning buzzed in Megan's mind. A bully who could twist a girl's arm until she screamed with pain, or a bully with a gun—there was one thing they had in common. Megan knew what that was and how to protect herself from it.

"Yes," she said in a small voice. "I'm afraid of you."

He smiled, his pride intact, and she could see him relax just a little.

"You're a dangerous man," she continued, "and probably very smart, too."

"That's right," he said. "I was smart enough to get away from that stupid marshal. They'll be hunting for me clear down Texas way, and here I am, with a full belly, just bidin' my time until I figure it's safe to start out again."

Megan could see Nelda wiping Emma's face with a damp cloth. She had to keep Napes's attention away from them and, at the same time, give herself a chance to think. The best thing to do right now, she decided, was to keep him talking.

"Tell me how you got away," she asked, and he obliged,

bragging in detail about his accomplishments. It was all Megan could do to nod approvingly as he described robberies, beatings, and destruction that made her sick to think about.

The puppies, wanting to be free from their box, began to yip, and the children grew restless, Thea whimpering for her mother. As Napes scowled in their direction, Megan picked up the nearest book, *Aesop's Fables*. "I'll give this to the children to look at," she said. Quickly she brought it to them, whispering, "Please, please be quiet!"

With wide eyes they stared at her, and Teddie reached for the book.

"Will you read to us about the fox?" he asked.

"In a little while," Megan said. She walked back to Napes, excited by the idea that had come to her.

The story Teddie wanted was her own favorite, about the conceited crow and the flattering fox.

*Well, Mr. Aesop,* Megan thought, *I know what to do with that story of yours. At least, I'm going to try. If I'm the fox, let's see if Mr. Napes will oblige by being the crow.*

Megan sat on the floor, just out of reach of Cully Napes's long legs and thick boots. "You must be very brave," she told him.

"Of course I am," he snarled.

"Tell me some of the things you've done."

"Why not," he said and preened just as the vain crow had done when the fox had tried to flatter her into dropping the piece of cheese he wanted.

He went on to brag about his exploits. Megan nodded and smiled, trying to look interested.

When he paused, she said, "I think you're almost as daring as the mountain men and the scouts in the West. I've heard lots of stories about them."

"Don't believe everything you hear. A lot of it's made-up braggin'," he snapped, and his eyes became narrow slits.

*Why, he's jealous of them*, Megan thought. *That's all to the good.* "I don't think it's just bragging," she said. "Why, I've heard that those men can aim their guns at the smallest of targets and hit them every time. I don't believe that anyone could shoot as well as they do—not even you."

Napes's feet and the two front legs of the chair hit the floor with a bang. "You're wrong about that! With this Remington .44 I can hit anything—or anyone—I want!"

Megan shrugged. "That's hard to believe."

"Are you calling me a liar?"

She was terrified that she'd gone too far. Gulping through the tightness in her throat, she stammered, "I'd never call you that, Mr. Napes, but it's only reasonable to want some proof." He opened his mouth to speak, but Megan rattled on. "If you were to stand on the front step, I bet you couldn't shoot well enough to hit the tips of the lower branches on the cottonwood tree near the road."

Megan scrambled to get out of the way as Napes leapt to his feet. "I'll show you I can!" He strode to the front door and threw it open.

Megan was right behind him, pointing to the tree. "That lower limb—can you hit it?"

Napes stood on the front step, readied his gun, raised it, and fired. The tip of the branch snapped off with a crack.

He chuckled and said, "I told you I was a good shot."

"How about that higher branch?" Megan asked.

He loaded the gun with ball, powder, and cap from the pouch at his belt, and again hit his mark.

"But how about over there? And there?" Megan kept an eye on the pouch.

Each time Napes took off the tip of the branch he was aiming at, until finally Megan said, "I'll admit, you're very good, but I don't think you can hit the top of the tree. Look—it's moving in the breeze. Nobody could hit it."

"Yeah? Just watch me." He held open the empty pouch and swore under his breath. "I'm out of ammunition," he said. "Stay right here. I'll get some from my saddlebags."

Megan waited until Napes had gone a few steps toward the barn. Then she snatched the Henry rifle from its place behind the coatrack and aimed it at him. "Stop," she said, "and turn around."

"What are you—" he barked, but his voice died away as he saw the gun.

"Don't you dare to move," she shouted. "You do what I tell you to do, or I'll shoot you. I'm a good shot, too."

"Listen, little girl," he began in a wheedling tone, but Megan interrupted.

"Throw your gun over here," she said. "Throw it inside the house." As he hesitated she added, "I've already counted to two, and I'm not going to count past three."

She stepped aside, and he slung his gun into the open doorway. She heard it slide and skitter across the wooden floor.

"Now," she said, "turn your back to me and lie flat on your face on the ground."

"I can't do that! It's too cold," he whined.

"You won't be there long," she said. "Only till the marshal gets back. And remember, I'll keep this gun on you the whole time. If you move even once, I'll shoot you." Her heart was beating so fast and loud she could hear it. "Be quick, now! Lie down on the ground as I told you to!"

Slowly he got to his knees, then lay down flat. She shivered, hoping she'd be able to keep her hold on the

**143**

heavy gun, wondering what she would do if Napes challenged her. She knew she couldn't shoot him. She couldn't shoot anyone. She just hoped he wouldn't guess that.

"Megan." Mrs. Parson spoke softly near her right ear, but Megan didn't dare take her eyes off Napes. "I don't know what to do. I can't let you stay here alone, but Emma needs me. Megan, do you understand? Emma is in labor!"

Megan took a quick breath. "Go to Emma," she whispered. "Trust me. I'll keep this man from causing any more harm."

"I'll take Emma to the bedroom," Mrs. Parson said, "and tell the children they must stay in the living room and play with the puppies. Oh, dear! If only—"

Megan's hands trembled, and she took a firmer grip on the gun. "Will Emma be all right?" she asked. But Mrs. Parson had gone inside.

Megan's hands were shaking so that she had a hard time keeping the rifle steady. Emma had to come through this with no harm! The baby, too! No matter what!

Cully Napes began to whimper. "You can't let the marshal arrest me. This whole business—that trouble in the tavern—it wasn't my fault."

"Stop it!" Megan shouted at Napes, her fears for Emma, for all of them, exploding in a burst of fury. "Of course it was your fault! And all the trouble you've caused here— that's your fault, too, and no one else's!"

Shocked, Megan gasped at what she had just said. For once she had blamed someone other than the gypsy or herself.

Emma's words came to mind: "Isn't trusting in your own good mind better than hiding behind a gypsy woman's silly superstition?"

"Hiding? From what?" Megan remembered how puzzled she had been. But now, a flame of rage at Napes burning her chest, she began to understand.

Napes barely stirred, but Megan yelled at him. "Don't you dare move! Unless you want to be shot!"

"I ain't moving!" he complained and began to mutter, "You can't shoot me. I didn't do nothin'."

"Oh, yes, you did!" Megan shot back, exulting in her anger. She carefully steadied the rifle. She had no time to think now about anything but Cully Napes. She could only stand there, keeping Napes at bay, ignoring his mumbled curses and threats, and praying that Ben would return soon.

# 15

By the time the men returned, the sun was pale fire splattered across the western sky, and shadows had turned into dark fingers that crawled quickly across the land.

Megan turned the rifle over to Ben and sank to the step, her legs too weak to hold her up. The marshal took his prisoner into custody. He roped Napes's arms to his sides and tied him to one of the supports in the barn for safekeeping until morning, when the two of them could set out for the jail in the county seat.

Finally Megan felt Ben's strong arms lifting her to her feet. "Oh, Ben—Emma," she said. "The baby's on the way."

"Nelda told me," Ben said. "I hurried inside first thing, to make sure that no one had been injured."

"Will she be all right?" Megan couldn't seem to stop shivering.

"Yes, of course," Ben answered, but his face was tight with worry.

Will clapped a hand on Ben's shoulder. "Women take

charge of these things," he said. "It's up to us to stay out of their way and wait. Believe me, they know what they're doing."

They walked into the house, the marshal following, and Megan said, "Emma had started a pot of soup. It should be ready."

"Good." The marshal patted his stomach. "I could use a hot meal."

Megan looked up at Ben timidly. "Please, could I talk to Emma first?"

"I don't know," Ben said helplessly. "Maybe after the baby gets here."

"Oh, please!" Megan begged. "Just for a minute?"

Ben thought a moment, then said, "It won't hurt to ask." He knocked at the door to their bedroom and talked in a low voice to Nelda. Finally he turned and smiled at Megan. "Emma wants to see you, too," he said. "Go on in. Nelda says she's resting comfortably right now."

Megan ran into the room and dropped to her knees by Emma's side. Emma, flushed and damp with perspiration, smiled and said, "You look so worried, Megan. Don't be afraid. Everything is going to be fine."

"The baby?"

"Even though it wasn't supposed to arrive for another two weeks, it's a large baby, and I'm sure it's old enough to be strong and healthy when it's born." She patted Megan's arm. "You were so brave, and I'm proud of you."

Megan sighed. "I was terribly afraid. And I told Mr. Napes I would shoot him." She shuddered. "I wouldn't have. I couldn't. I had to make him think so, though, so I lied to him."

"You told that lie to save us. Don't let it bother your conscience."

Megan laid her head against Emma's arm and held her hand tightly. "I did give some thought to all the things you told me about bad luck and the gypsy," she said, "and I think I understand now. You were right, the gypsy woman was an excuse I could hide behind. I could let myself get good and angry at the gypsy for making me a bad penny, and then I wouldn't have to be angry at anyone else. A lot of unhappy things have happened, and it was easy to blame the gypsy for all of them."

"It's not wrong to get angry," Emma said.

"I know that now. I was very angry at Cully Napes." Megan paused, a smile flickering on her lips. "It felt good. It helped give me the strength to keep that heavy rifle aimed at him."

For a moment Megan paused, and when she spoke again her voice was softer. "I guess deep inside I was angry when Da died. And I was angry with Mike for being a pickpocket and angry at Ma for sending us away. But I love them. I couldn't—couldn't—"

She raised her head and smiled into Emma's eyes. "I have learned this much," she said. "There's more to getting to where you're going than just knowing there's a road. Will you help me with the rest?"

"Oh, Megan," Emma said, twisting to wrap her arms around Megan. "I love you dearly."

Megan snuggled joyfully into Emma's hug. "After the baby comes, there's something I want to give you," she murmured. "It's the drawing Mr. Cartwright made."

"But that's your treasure," Emma protested.

"That's why I want you to have it," Megan said.

Emma beamed. "Oh, Megan, what a wonderful gift!"

Suddenly Emma released her hold on Megan and lay back, panting, her eyes closed as she gripped the edge of the quilt.

Megan sat back on her heels, frightened. "Emma?" she whispered.

Mrs. Parson said, "Don't worry, Megan." She helped Megan to her feet. "Suppose you dish up supper for the others. That's the best thing you can do to help right now."

"Are you sure she's all right?"

"Positive."

Megan did as she was told, glowing with the warmth of Emma's beautiful words: "I love you dearly."

*And I love you, Emma*, Megan said over and over to herself. *You and Ben and the baby*. She prayed with all her might that the baby would be strong and healthy. And she prayed for Emma each time she heard sounds from the bedroom. Time moved slowly. Why was the wait so long?

Later, much later, after everyone had eaten and Megan was carrying a stack of empty bowls to be washed, she heard a baby's cry. The tin bowls and spoons clattered to the floor.

"The baby!" she gasped.

Everyone stared wide-eyed at the closed door until they heard Nelda shout, "It's a healthy little boy!"

Ben grinned broadly as the marshal and Will clapped him on the back and shouted congratulations. Megan grabbed Thea's hands and spun her around and around, laughing and shouting.

It seemed to take forever before the bedroom door opened and Nelda said, "Ben, Megan, you can come in now."

Megan tiptoed into the room just behind Ben. Emma was propped against the pillows, holding the baby, who was wrapped in a small blanket, in her arms. Ben stooped to kiss Emma, and she pulled back a corner of the blanket to exhibit the tiny red face.

Megan laughed with delight. The baby looked so much

**149**

like Petey when he was born, red and wrinkled, with a nose no bigger than a round button. "He's beautiful and wonderful!" she murmured.

Emma reached over to clasp Megan's hand and looked up at Ben. "Now we have a daughter *and* a son to love!"

Ben put an arm around Megan, and she snuggled against him, but Emma's eyes began to sparkle with mischief.

"You know how hard it always is for me to wait for Christmas," she said to Ben. She nuzzled the top of her son's fuzzy head. "We received an early Christmas present. Now it should be Megan's turn."

"Emma," he protested with a laugh, but Emma paid no attention.

"Megan, look in the chest—the top drawer." As Megan did, Emma directed, "See the bundle wrapped in brown paper? Take it out and open it. It's yours."

Megan carefully unwrapped the paper to find a cloth doll with black button eyes and an embroidered smile. Dressed in a pink flowered dress with a white apron, she was the most beautiful doll Megan had ever seen. She was the only doll Megan had ever held.

As Megan looked at Emma, she couldn't find the words to tell her all that was in her heart. But Emma seemed to understand.

"Merry Christmas, little daughter," she said.

Tenderly Megan cradled the doll in the same way that Emma held her baby. It was almost Christmas, and Megan knew there'd be times during the holiday when she'd ache for her brothers and sisters and Ma. But she had Ben and Emma and the new little baby in her life now, and she loved them just as dearly as they loved her.

She hugged the doll and grinned back at Emma. "It's a *very* merry Christmas!" Megan said.

\*　　\*　　\*

As Grandma closed the journal Jennifer sighed. "I know how Megan must have felt. I'd hate to be away from my family at Christmas, especially if I hadn't heard from them and wondered what they were doing."

"Megan had heard from them," Jeff said. "Remember the letters from her mother and Mike and Frances?"

Jennifer wrapped her arms around her legs, hugging her knees. "But not Danny and Peg," she said. She turned to Grandma. "Why didn't they write to Megan?"

"Maybe they didn't know how," Jeff said.

"But someone could help them. What about their new mother, Grandma? Couldn't she write a letter for them?"

Grandma shook her head. "I'm afraid not."

Both Jennifer and Jeff stared at her. "Why not?"

Grandma got to her feet. "It would take too long to tell you now," she said. "That's another story."

Jennifer studied her grandmother with suspicion. "Can't you even give us a hint? Did Danny and Peg get into trouble?"

"Yes," Grandma said. "Some of it was of Danny's own making, but the attempted kidnapping—well, of course that wasn't his fault."

Jennifer jumped up. "Kidnapping! Can't you tell us more about it?"

Grandma looked at her watch. "We've got time to make a trip to the grocery store before I put a roast in the oven. Want to come along?"

"I do," Jeff said.

"I do, too," Jennifer answered, "but you didn't answer my question."

Grandma smiled. "I'll answer it. I'll tell you everything that Frances Mary wrote in her journal about Danny and Peg—but not until tomorrow."

## About the Author

JOAN LOWERY NIXON is the acclaimed author of more than sixty fiction and non-fiction books for children and young adults. She is a three-time winner of the Mystery Writers of American Edgar Award and the recipient of many Children's Choice awards. Her popular books for young adults include the first two books in the Orphan Train Quartet, *A Family Apart* and *Caught in the Act*, *The Kidnapping of Christina Lattimore*, *The Specter*, and *The Seance*. She was moved by the true experiences of the children on the nineteenth-century orphan trains to research and write the Orphan Train Quartet.

Mrs. Nixon and her husband live in Houston, Texas.

Copy 1

NIX                          Copy 1

Nixon, Joan Lowery      # 3

The Orphan Train Quartet
In the Face of Danger

| OCT 16 '91 | DATE DUE | |
|---|---|---|
| OCT 24 '91 | MAY 2 2 1992 | |
| NOV 7 '91 | JAN 19 '93 | |
| NOV 21 '91 | MAR 15 '93 | |
| DEC 6 '91 | MAY 13 '93 | |
| DEC 1 9 1991 | | |
| JAN 2 1992 | | |
| JAN 3 0 1992 | | |
| Vol - Van der Vote | | |
| APR 1 1992 | | |
| Fond Vol | | |